The Sage of
Waterloo

The Sage of Waterloo

∷ *A Tale* ∷

Leona Francombe

W. W. NORTON & COMPANY

New York • *London*

For information about permission to reproduce selections from this
book, write to Permissions, W. W. Norton & Company, Inc.,
500 Fifth Avenue, New York, NY 10110

For information about special discounts for bulk purchases, please
contact W. W. Norton Special Sales at specialsales@wwnorton.com
or 800-233-4830

Manufacturing by Courier Westford
Book design by Abbate Design/Judith Stagnitto Abbate
Production manager: Anna Oler

Library of Congress Cataloging-in-Publication Data

Francombe, Leona.
The Sage of Waterloo : a tale / Leona Francombe.—First edition.
    pages cm
ISBN 978-0-393-24691-9 (hardcover)
I. Title.
PS3606.R3754S25 2015
813'.6—dc23

                                    2014044186

W. W. Norton & Company, Inc.
500 Fifth Avenue, New York, N.Y. 10110
www.wwnorton.com

W. W. Norton & Company Ltd.
Castle House, 75/76 Wells Street, London W1T 3QT

1 2 3 4 5 6 7 8 9 0

For Peter, my sage,

and in honor of Mum and Dad

Yea, the coneys are scared by the thud of hoofs,
And their white scuts flash at their vanishing
        heels . . .

—THOMAS HARDY,
"The Field of Waterloo"

The conflict is there petrified; it lives, it dies;
it was but yesterday. The walls are still in their
final throes; the holes are wounds; the breaches
are howling; the trees bend and shudder, as if
making an effort to escape.

—VICTOR HUGO
on visiting the site of
Hougoumont Farm after
the Battle of Waterloo

Preface

*T*he ancient farmstead of Hougoumont sits
beneath the ridge near Waterloo where, on June
17, 1815, the Duke of Wellington amassed his
troops. He garrisoned the farm that evening and was determined to hold on to it, bringing in supplies and shoring up
defenses throughout that rain-drenched night. The next day,
French soldiers under the command of Jérôme Bonaparte,
Napoleon's brother, mounted no fewer than seven attacks on
the gates and walls of Hougoumont. What initially had
been intended as a skirmish raged all day, sapping Napoleon
of troops needed elsewhere.

Combat was brutal, often hand-to-hand. The chateau

and several outbuildings were set ablaze by French artillery; the North Gate was momentarily breached, then retaken; heavy wooden doors are, to this day, riddled with musket shot. The British Guards and their German allies in the woods eventually prevailed. But the cost in blood was staggering: within eight hours, six thousand men from both sides were either dead or wounded. This remote Belgian farm would turn out to be pivotal to the outcome of the Battle of Waterloo, and had the French taken it, history might have followed a very different route.

Few had heard of Hougoumont before that tumultuous day. The estate was the seat of an obscure Belgian aristocrat and rather isolated, though it was prosperous, with a small chateau, formal walled garden in the French style, chapel, gardener's house and various outbuildings for animals and grain. Fine dining had no doubt been a daily ritual. As recipes for rabbit and pigeon dishes were—and still are—numerous in Belgian cuisine, both species, along with a decent onion patch, would have been nurtured on the property with the dinner table in mind. So there were almost certainly rabbits at Hougoumont at the time of the Battle of Waterloo.

L. Francombe
Brussels, Belgium

The Sage of
Waterloo

1

All early memories are close-ups, aren't they? A blade of grass; a clump of earth; the underside of someone's tail. For me, it was Grandmother's flank. My nose still seeks that smell: a sour-sweet, heady brew of hay, dung and humidity, all alchemized in the crucible of old age. There was a decaying floral note to her perfume, too, hence her name: Old Lavender. She was very large and of no particular color—a mix of dull grays and browns, I suppose, though I'd never really thought about it. One never really thinks about such things when it comes to close family members. All the qualities we criticize in others—fatness, dullness, ugliness, smell—somehow don't matter so much in relatives.

Old Lavender possessed a different set of attributes altogether, some of them as unpalatable as those listed above, but her temperament was such that, in view of the strength of her kick, no one dared to criticize anything about her. She spent her days crouched in a hollow against the wire fence, eyes half shut, contemplating the infinite. One ear would lie flat against her neck, the other pointing to the sky. She always sat like that. We suspected this was how she gathered her information: one ear searching the heavens for signals while the other acted as a sort of ground. *The most interesting things in life cannot be seen, William,* Grandmother often told me, which made her sky-combing all the more intriguing.

No one could say how long Old Lavender had lived in the colony. She was grandmother to at least ten generations, and while other relatives disappeared over the years at the farmer's whims, or those of Moon, the invisible arbiter of our kind, she had always been permitted to stay. No one dared to cross her. She was just too big, for one thing. And of course, there was that smell . . .

But perhaps I ought to start at the beginning. Not out of any logic, but because, for some reason, the beginning is getting clearer and clearer all the time, as if I'm approaching the end of the route we rabbits call the Hollow Way: a delightfully sheltered avenue smelling of damp earth and rot. The route is wider at this point, as it happens. Trees overhead provide the perfect balance of light and shade. And you can see quite far in both directions from here (though forward motion is, of course, still the preferred kind). There are many soft hillocks and hollows along this part of the Way on which one can rest and look back, and I suggest that you do this, too, because the view behind is as clear as the view ahead, and offers some valuable lessons besides.

Our route thus offers up a curious sort of map: a path forward, but only decrypted by the path behind. I imagine the landmarks along our Way are familiar to you, too—they're more or less standard on your typical life journey, I think: odd family members; dubious trysts; providence; bliss; disaster. The Hollow Way of my story, however, is unique in that, along with a particularly odoriferous grandmother, it also takes in the Battle of Waterloo. If you think that such a tale is rather exceptional for a simple rodent, you'd be wrong.

For in fact, strictly speaking I'm a lagomorph, not a rodent, and proud of it.

Here I find myself, then, arrived at a pleasant, grassy knoll, and with your indulgence I shall look back and tell you what I see.

∴

W e rabbits begin and end our lives in the earth, which may seem a vaguely circular progression, but I must hasten to say that we're not chained to an endless wheel of existence the way certain human sects are. I've heard that some people keep going round and round until the end of time, reincarnated as a fly, a reptile, someone's uncle, or, if you're terribly unlucky and happen to find yourself at Waterloo, as Napoleon. Moon can be louche at times, but he would never preside over such a dreary worldview.

Our philosophy is less hectic. We follow the Way at the speed it unfolds—no faster, no slower. This is very important. We are taught from infancy that any effort to adjust this speed is fruitless and can lead to ruin. Therefore we leap, graze, idle and cogitate according to a rhythm pulsing deep within us, like an essential organ. When things start to seem vaguely familiar, and then suddenly look very much like home, we take one, final step. And what a step it is!

Take it, they say, and you enter the greenest, spring-iest, most sublime meadow of all. We know without question when we're on the right road to this place.

Waterloo is where I was born, and where I spent the first three years of my life. Well, techni-cally it wasn't Waterloo itself but the ancient Bra-bant farm of Hougoumont, one of the iconic battle sites situated in the fields a few kilometers farther up the Chaussée de Waterloo. In 1815, this long, forested avenue funneled weary streams of human-ity back and forth between the battlefield and the city—between destiny and deliverance. Their pas-sage was perilous, the thoroughfare often impass-able. Where the city of Brussels has now expanded into tony suburbs, there were once deep woods, isolated hamlets and a pavement so rutted after heavy rains that wagons often remained stuck for days, or were simply abandoned by the side of the road. Thick undergrowth pressed in on both sides, and in the forest beyond, deserters from the battle found ample shelter . . . as did plunderers. Cottages and inns all along the *chaussée* stood empty in the face of a rumored French advance.

Today the plunderers are gone, thank heavens. But go past the fast-food emporiums and super-markets, cross over the Brussels ring road and suddenly, just beyond the electronics store, all the clamor of traffic and shopping gives way to a zone of silence, as if 1815 were not so very long ago after all. No one can miss it, this invisible boundary. Commerce stops dead at its feet. Venture on: when you spot the curious, conical hill with a statue on top—the Lion's Mound—you'll know you've entered the great battlefield itself: a wide, windy vacuum; the "*morne plaine*" of Victor Hugo. And indeed, beneath the winter barley, the clover, and the lumpen celeriac heads shrunken like mummies, this dreary plain is at its heart a tomb.

Cross the fields to your right and there, in a wooded valley, you'll find the farm I knew as home. Outbuildings and a gardener's house doze against a ragged hem of farmland. If you just stumble across Hougoumont, the scene is quite unremarkable: delapidated walls without ornament; encroaching weeds; the rusting remnants of farming life.

Until you see the three chestnuts.

At first you wonder why someone hasn't taken them down. Two are dead, the third not far behind them. They look like freaks—like alien carcasses stripped of their skin. Then you realize that they're over three hundred years old, and the only remaining witnesses to the fighting, and you understand. Place your hand on one of them—even on a dead one: you'll detect a pulse.

Hougoumont is . . . dear me, where are the words? It's a mute place, you see, but with such startling eloquence. Perhaps the fact that few visitors to the battlefield even know it exists fosters the air of an unopened message. Physically speaking, it's a ruin: a decaying farmstead of brick and sandstone in perfect complicity with the land. The other, less tangible things are far more difficult to describe. Go there yourself and you'll feel it: the knowing wind; the trees scarred as leviathans; and a strange sort of peace that isn't peaceful at all but alert with memory and other, less palatable phenomena. Sometimes, when the wind comes off the eastern fields, it's as if a worn curtain is shifting, and through a tear in the fabric you can see something unimaginable for such a sleepy backwater.

I was happy at Hougoumont. The last farmer to live there was not like the aristocrats who had once owned the chateau (there was no more chateau—the French had shelled it). He raised cattle, and seemed far less interested in rabbit and pigeon dishes than his predecessors. He was, thank heavens, a frozen-food sort of man, and thus our existence was blissfully irrelevant.

We were cared for by a local boy, Emmanuel, an oafish giant who neglected us mainly because he could never remember whether he had fed us or not. He also flatly refused to come to the farm after dark. If other chores kept him busy elsewhere and the twilight began to deepen, he would just toss a few grains over the fence to us and pedal off on his bicycle—and at an impressive speed, too, for such a pudgy fellow. Perhaps, like many simpletons, his raw senses made up for lack of brainpower; perhaps he could intuit the unrest at Hougoumont even better than we could, and felt it begin to stir at dusk.

Emmanuel was too benign to cause any intentional harm. We even suspected that the only reason the farmer kept us on was to give him something to do. Maybe because the boy seemed so unloved, we developed a love for him ourselves, though I don't think he ever noticed, to be honest. But as I learned only years later, such a thing should never play a role in the offering of love.

My crèche was the humblest of rabbit pens. The run stood next to a dovecote—a hexagonal Victorian frippery abandoned years ago—and was enclosed by rusting chicken wire nailed to a fence and strung overhead in a roof of sorts, although any predator worthy of the name could probably have found a way in. Grass once grew in the enclosure, but so long ago that my grandmother was the only one who remembered it. For the rest of us, hard, unyielding earth was our world.

The run was furnished with a makeshift hutch the farmer had cobbled together with fallen beams from the old granary. Whenever he remembered, Emmanuel herded us into this fetid abode before sundown; if he forgot, or the approaching darkness scared him off, most of us knew to go in by ourselves. The jaws and beaks of predators, real or imagined, loomed large in the country night.

Beyond the dovecote we could glimpse the old, wounded Hougoumont: the original gardener's house, stables, cobbled courtyard and battle-worn doors, all creeping with mold and cracking in the tight, dank grasp of time. Only the tiny chapel had been restored, its new roof sloping like a nun's cap, a remnant of the vanished chateau still attached to one end. From our grandmother we'd learned where in the courtyard the famous haunted well had been. According to legend, three hundred corpses were thrown down it just after the fighting in an effort to ward off disease, and later, long after any poor, still-breathing soul could have uttered them, unearthly cries still issued from the depths.

⁝

Hougoumont's restless past was our only company. I'm not speaking of haunted wells here; or of trifling amusements to relieve boredom.

You see, our pen overlooked what used to be the formal chateau gardens, witness to the slaughter of 1815. What lingered there was powerful enough even for human nerve endings to register. You would hardly believe it now, though, from the lush expanse of meadow where the gardens had been, and the cows serenely grazing there. We barely believed it ourselves.

Until we were taught otherwise . . . until we could read the air.

But what temptations drifted in from that paradise before we'd learned to read! Our young hearts overflowed with bounty. Poplar leaves flashed like coins in the breeze. Wood pigeons cooed from across the valley. On spring twilights, blackbirds staged their pearly evensong in trees tilted like wizards. We would press against the chicken wire and listen, staring out across the meadow all the way to the eastern wall where, through a breach, there stretched an ocean of space that used to be the old orchard but was now open farmland. Cloistered as we were, this green sea was our own Elysium—our Untried—and like anybody's fantasy, made even more enchanting by the knowledge that we could never go there.

Each fantasy carries a stain, however.

Something other than enchantment dwelled beneath those lush grasses; something that made the tips of our ears go cold. Our senses, exquisitely tuned, could catch unearthly signals as easily as spiderwebs catch floating down, so it took very little effort for us to hear the Hougoumont meadow whispering in its sleep. Try as we might, we younger members of the colony couldn't read those signals properly—not as Old Lavender could—though the whispering often kept us awake . . . that, and the insistent, rhythmic tapping of a beech branch against the south wall.

"Don't forget," Grandmother cautioned. "Two hundred years ago, the meadow was hardly untried." (She was generally considered to be an expert on Waterloo.) "It was a soaked, bloody sponge, and nobody's fantasy. It wasn't even a meadow back then, you know. It was a French garden: orange trees, roses, geraniums—everything was in full flower during the battle. Corpses were piled six high, over there, against the wall." Out of politeness, we tried not to stare where she was indicating, though of course we threw avid glances that way.

As you can imagine, Old Lavender's comments cast a shadow over our Elysium. But it's a curious thing about shadows: They're not what you remember about a beloved place . . . about home. You remember the sweet smell of woodland decay; the tilled earth on the wind; the blackbirds' cantata in the valley. You don't remember stains. At least, you push them into a dark corner and rarely visit them there.

It was clear that Hougoumont was coming to a sad, lingering end. It had reached a crossroads of sorts even before I'd left, its future as uncertain as our own. I'm not even sure how much longer the others in the colony stayed on after I was gone. One more crisp, silent winter, perhaps? A final, aromatic spring? The farmer might even have passed away by now, and the place gone to ruin. I can barely contemplate what the fate of my family would have been then, with the main gates locked and Emmanuel, even if he'd remembered, not being able to get in. (The French had had enough trouble, if you recall.) I can only hope that the blackbirds organized some kind of requiem.

∴

I am no longer young. I'll be eleven in a few months, which not only requires math well beyond my skills to calculate in human years, but also obliges me to press on with my storytelling. Those of you who are already experiencing the adventure of aging may have discovered that this part of the journey does not only entail unexpected dips and fissures in the road, aches in the limbs, problems reaching those hard-to-clean areas (Old Lavender gave them up early on) and so forth. No, there's much more to it, as it turns out. One great plus is the subtle tuning that takes place, as if Moon—or whatever you prefer to call the tuner—were drawing gently tighter a hitherto merrily quivering string, with the perceptible and rather heady effect of purer tone and sweeter echo. (Other interesting effects, presumably, are to follow.) At the same time, one feels a certain lifting of the spirit and breadth of vision, as if—in my case, anyway—one were looking down at farm and family from the summit of the Lion's Mound. It's not surprising, therefore, that I can still picture fairly well the dramatis personae of my youth.

Jonas, a distant cousin, was a rash, handsome buck infamous for his preening, scheming and disreputable tail-chasing. When she was angry with him, Old Lavender called him Marshal Ney after Napoleon's hotheaded commander. It was meant as an insult. But what Grandmother didn't realize was that Jonas had actually been listening on the day she'd given the lecture on Ney, and the heroic bits had sunk in. She respected accuracy even more than she disliked Ney, so she had to give the Marshal his due. For example, she couldn't omit the fact that he'd been nicknamed "the bravest of the brave" for his cavalry charges, foolhardy though they'd been; or that five horses had been shot from under him and even that hadn't stopped him. Jonas was rather pleased, therefore, with Grandmother's insult.

Boomerang, a slightly crazed uncle, had the obscure habit of throwing himself sideways against the barrier, bouncing off at ever-more-interesting angles. The gentle addling of the brain that resulted was part of his charm.

Caillou was the runt (his name, fittingly, meant "pebble"). He was always underfoot, and a typical runt mainly because there was absolutely nothing of note to say about him.

And then there was Berthe . . . poor, homely Berthe, a placid doe, and rather saintly in the respect that she vowed to reject all suitors until she found her true soul mate. To my great chagrin, her glance occasionally fell my way. I don't mean any disrespect here. Berthe was sweet, and so earnestly eager to please. But she had no interest whatsoever in history. She could never be bothered to check her facts: she insisted, for example, that the Battle of Waterloo had occurred on June 15, 1818, and not on June 18, 1815. (Maybe she was dyslexic.) She didn't even know what had happened at Hougoumont. So what would we talk about during those long winter nights?

Spode was the elder statesman of the colony. He was an archivist par excellence, collecting tidbits of information from passing wildlife or tourists and codifying his findings one by one with little, officious sniffs. There were few topics about which he couldn't—or didn't—discourse, which was one of the reasons that he sought out my grandmother for conversation.

Spode had escaped once, a feat that offset his general stuffiness somewhat. He was gone for three days, coming back to us in a porcelain soup tureen (alive, thank heavens), this being the only receptacle the farmer's wife had handy to capture him among her cabbages. Perhaps because of this impressive episode, Old Lavender designated Spode the colony's lookout. Whenever he wasn't engaged in research, therefore, he would patrol the perimeter of the enclosure like some aging fusilier, thumping his hind foot at any sign of danger. When he *was* engaged in research—which was most of the time—we were on our own.

Spode was fat and deliberate, with little brown spots on his jowls and a rather superior aspect that was tough to chew on, like dry corn husks. He occasionally embarked on philosophical discussions with Old Lavender, but she couldn't abide his airs, promptly turning her rump to him whenever she'd had enough. He always deferred to her, however. She was older than he, and her knowledge of Waterloo more comprehensive, so he usually ambled away with a sniff rather than enter into a full-blown argument with a creature who could have felled him with a single kick. Grandmother often referred to Spode as Bonaparte behind his back, which was sad, really, considering the flame he carried for her. He wasn't a bad sort. But we weren't about to cry *"Vive l'empereur!"* whenever he walked by, either.

Most of us followed the general rules that defined the Hollow Way. Yield. Bump ahead. No left turn. That sort of thing. It was a predictable sort of life, vigorously stamped with the colony's imprimatur: milling, eating, nudging, nipping, dozing . . . milling, eating, nudging, nip . . . You get the idea. That said, we were a democratic lot, never according privileges based on birth; always allowing freedom of religion, including complete denial of Moon, should that be one's bent; favoring merit-based opportunities (Jonas, for instance,

with his natural zeal and superior shoulder mus-
cles, was in charge of digging the hole under the
hutch). I would venture to say that we were probably some of the first unsung proponents of the
Napoleonic Code.

∴

Not all of us followed the rules, however. Jonas
had written his own set and was determined
to abide by them, no matter what the price. How
I envied him! Even though envy is against our
tenets. I was so dispiritingly hesitant and insecure.
I never took the initiative, despite the little spasm
of wildness that surfaced in me from time to time.
My kick was weak and my shoulders lacked tone.
It was impossible not to envy the impulsive, exu-
berant, good-looking Jonas. He was everything I
wanted to be.

He'd been working on a hole under the hutch for
some months, even boasting that his tunnel would
soon reach the south wall and he'd be remembered for generations to come as a great liberator
and risk-taker, all the while avoiding (naturally!)
the taint of infamy that still dogged Marshal Ney.
Jonas occasionally dug up old lead musket balls
as he worked, which further inflated his Napole-

onic ardor. It's said that approximately three and a half million bullets were fired during the Battle of Waterloo, which made it nigh impossible for an athletic rabbit like Jonas to dig a decent hole and *not* turn one up. According to the metal detector enthusiasts who regularly trawl the grounds of Hougoumont, you know which bullets are French and which are British by their weight: the former weigh twenty-two grams; the latter, thirty.

One twilight, just as we were filing indoors for the evening, Jonas lingered at his digging. Something had taken hold of him: a stray signal from the fields, perhaps, or more specifically, the scent of a wild doe. Whatever the temptation, he suddenly flung himself into the air as if electrified and tried to leap over the barrier, getting fouled on a sharp wire at the top. There he hung, a pitiful sight, bleeding badly.

We milled below in confusion, not knowing what to do. I milled the closest, awestruck by Jonas's momentous deed—by the grandeur of his suffering, and the dark uncertainty of his fate. I thought of my own wild spasms and realized how puny they were in comparison to Jonas's. I would never have the courage to act on them as he had.

Emmanuel forgot us that evening, as it hap-

pened (though even if he had turned up, he probably wouldn't have known what to do, either). Spode
was not on lookout duty, having been engaged all
day in an analysis of Marshal Grouchy's suitability
for leading Napoleon's right wing during the Waterloo campaign, so it was Old Lavender who offici-
ated. She delivered a thunderous thump against
the packed earth and then, to our shock, nipped
at our heels and ordered us all into the hutch posthaste, leaving Jonas to the predators. Was this his
ultimate Ney lesson? I wondered. Had the spirit of
the hotheaded commander at last come to rest at
Hougoumont?

Jonas hung there all night. His blood coursed
down the chicken wire and left dark, spreading
stains in the dust. Moon must not have been far
away, however, because incredibly, come morning, my cousin hadn't succumbed to his wounds,
or been carried off by an owl as everyone had
expected. He was even still able to tell a few jokes.
But he paid for his rashness, just as Grandmother
said he would (though not as heavily as Ney, who
had lost the better part of a brigade).

After the farmer had disentangled Jonas,
and all the fur on his stomach had been shaved
and the wound sewn up, he just wasn't the same

Jonas anymore. Some of the hot air had definitely leaked out.

Then something strange happened. After his near-death experience, Jonas started going around doing uncharacteristically selfless deeds, as if he were trying to begin again as another rabbit. He let the others eat first instead of charging the dish—even giving priority to Caillou, who was universally tromped on; he didn't push his way into the hutch at night to get the best patch of hay. That sort of thing. Was this some kind of latter-day saintliness?

Grandmother didn't think so. She'd never trusted Jonas, old or new. "He's still the most unreliable scrap of fur I ever saw," she huffed. She also said that to qualify for sainthood, you have to give up the best patch of hay from your earliest days. Our species has to hit the ground running and not change course, she said. Therefore, you generally are what you are from birth onward. (She was definitely old school, that one.) I'm not so sure, myself. I think that we all deserve a second chance. Even Jonas. It's just that do-good*ees* have to realize that at least half of all do-good*ing* benefits the do-good*er*, which was definitely the case with Jonas and certainly not a crime in itself, but also not, strictly speaking, a means to sainthood. I have to say that I missed the old Jonas—the incorrigible cad in the grand French tradition; the carefree spirit I so longed to be. The ladies missed him, too.

2

Visitors occasionally poked around the farm in those days looking for evidence of the famous battle. They would leave flowers against the chapel wall, and run their hands wonderingly over the pockmarks in the doors. Their pilgrimage invariably led them on a path from the courtyard to the meadow, passing by the dovecote along the way. Generally, we were overlooked, which was understandable. The atmosphere grows heavy in that part of the farm; history quickens. No one expects to see rabbits.

I don't remember when, exactly, I first set eyes on the two ladies. They'd been coming for years, according to Grandmother. One had snowy hair, the other silver, and from a distance they looked like winter by moonlight. They had a singular aura about them, as if they'd been charmed, and drifted so softly about the place that it seemed the air itself was dictating their movements. They wore rubber boots, even in summer, and I don't think there was a bullet hole or boggy corner they didn't know by heart.

Armed with maps and guides, the ladies would wander around the farm for hours at a time, pausing frequently to consult their material and read each other passages aloud. Their preferred author was Charlotte Eaton, the Englishwoman who had found herself in Brussels on June 15, 1815—the eve of the Battle of Quatre Bras—and stayed abroad long enough to visit Hougoumont and other key sites a month later.

Most striking of all was that our lady visitors seemed to have found that restless Hougoumont harmonic, and instinctively followed it to the lodes of greatest passion: the loopholes; the North Gate; the vanished well; the chestnuts. It was remarkable, really. We'd always been taught that our senses were far more finely tuned to the pulse of

Hougoumont than those of people, but here they were, two human females who actually seemed to read the air. They would wander off, one without the other, and stand very still under some tree or other, simply looking up at the sky.

"Thank heavens for the Eaton ladies!" Old Lavender said, and the moniker stuck. "War desperately needs a female perspective. Why is the scourge of the entire human race always recounted by only half of it—and the guilty half, at that?"

The ladies sometimes lingered at the dovecote, where they could lean comfortably against the rail fence and peruse their guides. The sight of Old Lavender arrested them every time.

"What a huge rabbit!" one would exclaim, as if Grandmother had grown since their last visit.

"She looks like one of those rabbits in Oriental paintings," the other offered. "You know: the matriarch brooding off in one corner."

I've never been to a museum myself, so I can't say for sure if this description was accurate. But the idea haunted me. Doubtless an enigma cloaked Old Lavender, made weightier by certain events in her past that she kept to herself.

Another thing Grandmother kept to herself was the business of my own bloodline. She implied vaguely that it had taken a more circuitous route than her own, but again, failed to elaborate. I was the only white rabbit in the enclosure . . . that much anyone could grasp. It was also clear that somehow, through some obscure event, I was connected to Hougoumont's history in a way that others in the colony were not. I'd felt this distinction—or perhaps stigma is more accurate—for as long as I could remember.

Every two or three generations, a white rabbit was born in the colony. Sometimes this creature was pure white; sometimes it had various splashes of black on its coat, like me. Mystery dogged the carriers of this gene. Some believed it could be traced back two hundred years, to the chevalier's rabbits in the great barn. If this were true, one would naturally assume that there would have been at least one white rabbit that had survived the bombardment, though few small creatures could have made it through such a cataclysm. You would then have to take the scenario even further, and assume that at least one male and one female rabbit had been left in the Napoleonic hutch. And then the final supposition: that they had not been too traumatized to procreate.

It is indeed a strange sort of upheaval, not knowing one's origins, as if you've been cut loose from the natural order of things and left to float out of reach, and even simple givens, like day following night, cannot be relied upon.

∴

There must have been something worthwhile about my uniqueness, for I was the only one Old Lavender let sit beside her.

Her favorite spot was a dusty hollow at the northeast corner of the pen. Her routine never varied: She would first groom herself (the places she could still reach, that is). Then she would settle into the hollow gradually, methodically, shifting her rump back and forth, lower and lower, until she found the heart of the spot. Finally, she would lay one ear flat against her neck, cock the other one straight up and narrow her eyes.

Only then was I permitted to slink in.

Mutely, I would press myself against the warm cave between her thighbone and belly, listening to the tuneful plumbing of her digestion and staring out through the chicken wire in the general direction she was staring.

"You're like a bowl of water with a calm surface, William," Grandmother liked to say. "You can't see to the bottom of it. But you know it's deep."

Her description would sometimes come to mind as I sat beside her, pretending to feel watery and deep and naïvely trying to follow her thoughts. But as I looked out at the provocative, breezy wildness of the meadow, my bowl would invariably be far from calm, and a familiar restlessness would plague me that set up all sorts of ripples on the surface. Maybe Grandmother had noticed those ripples all along, and had named me William after Wellington's inexperienced ally, the Prince of Orange, who was generally well liked, but whose heroics at the Battle of Quatre Bras were still open to interpretation. *His* bowl had definitely had a few ripples . . . if not some large waves.

Sometimes Old Lavender would run her nose through my fur in the wrong direction, a gesture that usually infuriates a rabbit. But not me. I can still feel it to this day—the exciting novelty of it; the bracing discomfort. It took me ages to connect a curious lift in my thinking with this annoyance and grasp the underlying message: that too much comfort dampens the brain.

Every once in a while, Grandmother would open her eyes fully and say: "Try to imagine the unimaginable, William."

You could interpret that many ways, I suppose. But back then, I knew of only one way, and would dutifully try to imagine that bucolic farm and all the fragrant fields around it, running with blood.

And not just human blood, either, but the blood of every sort of wild creature who, until that terrible day two hundred years ago, had never questioned their rightful place in the universe.

I've reflected all my life on that rightful place, and on how precarious it really is; how, for instance, my hero, the Duke of Wellington, managed to make it through the entire three days of the Battle of Waterloo without so much as a bullet grazing him. "The finger of Providence was upon me," he was quoted as saying. That he could remain unscathed when practically all his personal staff were killed, wounded or had their horses shot from under them is one of history's great sleights of hand.

The question is: Whose hand?

No one, to my knowledge, has had the indelicacy to dispute Wellington's explanation of his good fortune. There he was, telescope in hand, riding back and forth for hours in the very thick of battle, encouraging, directing and animating, death ever at his elbow. His esteemed quartermaster-general, Sir William De Lancey, was blown from his horse by the wind of a cannonball *en ricochet* at the very moment when he was speaking to the Duke, suffering terrible injuries from which he would die a week later; the Earl of Uxbridge was shot in the leg in almost identical circumstances; Sir Alexander Gordon, a friend and aide-de-camp to the Duke, had a leg amputated and died in Wellington's own camp bed. Even nonbelievers might make an exception and take Wellington at his word.

.·.

After a period of reflection—several days or so—Old Lavender would lecture to the enclosure at large. The place was crowded: we were unable to eat, groom, fornicate or daydream more than about a foot away from someone else, so she had a decent captive audience. Not that we objected. She mined her Waterloo passion for treasures that were exclusively ours for the taking.

It was a subject none of us could avoid, of course, living as we did against the very earth that had shook with the conflict, and breathing air still dense with souls. Like the rest of us, Old Lavender couldn't escape her destiny as a small creature, so her brand of history had mainly to do with small things.

"Our point of view is a gift," she said. "We understand essential minutiae, in our species and in humans: unease in a voice or gesture; electricity sparked by panic or excitement; signals betraying doubt, joy, grief. And don't forget the rich realm of smell. What an encyclopedia that is! Any one of you could have picked up Napoleon's stress on the eve of battle." Grandmother went on to say that Napoleon's very pores had exuded the sort of anxiety that even the dullest animal wit can pick up. His human entourage, however, could only go by less subtle pointers: loud, agitated talking, and orders issued with great vehemence; constant snuff-taking, and the supreme confidence that he would be sleeping at the royal palace in Brussels after his victory.

History is in the details . . . How many times we were reminded of that! Pick the details that move you, we were instructed—the ones that speak to you, and arrest you. Then build your idea of history around them, for only then will it come alive.

My first lessons taught me the smallest pearls . . . so small that any serious pearl fisherman would have tossed them away. But through Old Lavender's eyes, these tiny treasures were like pebbles viewed through a drop of rain: color, size and clarity were all enhanced, transforming an insignificant scrap of stone into a jewel.

Observe closely, Grandmother said, adding: *but with passion*. And what a passionate stage she set! She was living proof that emotion can reside in the surliest, smelliest of vessels.

Clouds, mists, driving rain . . . annoying details, perhaps, but on the eve of Waterloo, our countryside had become the twilight of some despairing god. Higher forces were clearly circling . . . circling . . .

"It was peculiarly awful, that storm," Old Lavender said. "An omen, surely. Soldiers fell up to their necks in mud. It was only logical that Napoleon had to wait for things to dry a bit before he could move his artillery. Cannonballs need to deflect, after all, and not get bogged down. It was a fateful waste of time, though. Napoleon was four hours late to his own battle."

Don't wait for the mud to dry before you go ahead and do things was, therefore, one of Grandmother's classic aphorisms, along with: *You can always jump higher than you think you can,* referring to our ancestors in the chateau hutches, who may or may not have escaped the Hougoumont siege. Like most historical details, it depends on whom you ask.

It's a curious fact that no one knows at what time, exactly, the Battle of Waterloo began. Most historians think it was around eleven-thirty in the morning; Old Lavender thought it started at eleven. Her conviction was such that she could have told us it started at midnight and we would have believed her.

She would have been a natural film director, our grandmother, so sweeping was her vision.

The panorama she created spread to the farthest reaches of our fancy, and even with our eyes closed, we couldn't fathom its limits. Her images were only words, of course. But how they hummed through our waking hours and commandeered our dreams! She cast such a spell that we weren't sure what was real, and what imagined. We were kept awake by the smell of the wet, trampled barley the soldiers slept on the night before the battle. We felt the floor of the hutch shudder at Napoleon's magnificent cuirassiers, advancing at full gallop. We heard every strike of the village clock on that June morning—even counted them aloud until eleven, when we imagined the French guns thundering to life.

Now and then, Grandmother indulged Caillou with his favorite bedtime story. It's an elusive tale, and one with few hard facts: a French drummer boy survived the bloody siege of Hougoumont's North Gate. That's about it. Hardly enough, you would say, to fashion a decent bedtime story. But it was the kind of deceptive triviality that Grandmother so loved, because historians generally tossed it away like those careless pearl fishermen—even misrepresented it—not realizing what bounty they had missed. Old Lavender thus felt free to appropriate the treasure and do with it as she liked.

The drummer boy himself was never identified. He'd been led into the Hougoumont barn at the height of the battle by Private Matthew Clay, a British soldier who was hardly more than a boy himself at the time, and whose eyewitness account was widely quoted by the Eaton ladies. According to Clay, the drummer boy survived a skirmish at the South Gate, not the North. (Grandmother never understood how historians could be so remiss with their reading.)

No one knows what happened to the French boy after that. Was he an orphan? An impoverished urchin seeking adventure? Other youngsters had run off to war under such circumstances, after all. Did he ever make his way back to France, or even grow to manhood?

In the manner of the greatest teachers, Old Lavender placed the pearls before us but made us string and polish them ourselves. She was not without her opinions, though.

"He may have become a teacher, or a leader . . . even a philosopher," she offered. "He'd seen the slaughter at Hougoumont with an innocent's gaze, don't forget. Like your own." The comment made us look around the hutch at each other in a new, dawning way. "He could have helped chart another course for humanity, away from its morbid obsession with war."

Then her tone cooled, and her eyes revealed deeper significance: "Or he may have perished finding his way off the battlefield. Died of fever . . ." Her pause was exquisitely timed. "And become something else."

Our nerves sparked to life. Consider it: from such uncertainty does history take its oxygen. When the what, where, who, how and why of a historical event are known, then all the details are neatly recorded, entombed between the covers of a weighty book and stowed away on a shelf, only to be taken down some twenty years later when someone needs a doorstop. (A reasonable description of Spode, come to think of it.)

Whatever the details surrounding the mysterious drummer boy, we all sensed that there was something odd about him, as if he'd not quite signed off on his own drama . . . even centuries later. For my part, I secretly believed that providence had brushed against this incident (when not otherwise engaged with the Duke of Wellington, that is), making from it the sort of tantalizing, underwater gleam one can never bring to the surface.

Old Lavender embellished the story for Caillou, of course. She even became quite poetic, describing the boy's slight build, his tousled hair, and the large brown eyes that had missed nothing on that humid summer afternoon. The runt invariably dozed off before she'd finished. But the rest of us just weren't able to sleep, somehow. We would tune our ears warily to the wind outside the hutch, listening for the tap of stick against drum. There were all sorts of stray sounds in the Hougoumont night one couldn't always explain. Rhythmic tapping was just one of them.

∴

Mornings were reserved for pop quizzes: "What did Wellington have for breakfast?" (Hot, sweet tea and toast. Napoleon, by the way, took his breakfast on silver plate.) "Why was Napoleon such a poor rider?" (He slid around on the saddle too much, wearing holes in his breeches.) "How long was Generalfeldmarschall Gebhard Leberecht von Blücher pinned under his dead horse?" (Even longer than it takes to pronounce his name properly.) "What did they use to revive him? (Blücher, not the horse: gin and garlic.)

I had no difficulty building history around these nuggets. In fact, I often escaped into my creations completely, which was probably not what Grandmother had in mind, crusty realist that she was.

You see, all of her details moved me, arrested me, spoke to me . . . to the very depths of my soul.

I hardly knew which one to choose from. For guaranteed escape, Wellington was always a good bet, so I would track him eagerly as he rode about all day in his plain blue frock coat and bicorne hat, amazed at how such a mythmaker could subsist on just hot tea and toast. Then I would leave the Duke to his reconnoitering for a while and practice pronouncing *Generalfeldmarschall Gebhard Leberecht von Blücher.* I never really mastered it, despite all the hours spent trying, thereby gaining a much greater appreciation of the old Prussian general's predicament. (He was seventy-three at the time.) When those activities paled, I imagined myself boldly escaping from the Hougoumont barn during the fiercest of the fighting, leaping across the chateau garden through a blizzard of bullets, the finger of providence firmly upon me.

Sometimes, in the sanctum of the hollow, I stole a glance at the long-eared sphinx that was my grandmother and wondered how she could possibly know as much as she did. Anyone can stare for hours through a wire fence, after all, thinking about nothing much. But she had elevated patient observation to the highest art form; she listened, and deliberated, and had detected the unrest in that walled meadow long before any of us were born. It was obvious from her vast knowledge that she enjoyed privileged communion with something or other: Moon, perhaps. But he's a casual god as these things go, and I'm not sure he was all that keen on historical detail, to be honest, having been so spectacularly absent from one of history's most famous battles.

My theory is that Old Lavender used her cunning, and her extreme sensitivity, to glean and intuit. She could read shifts in the air; tremors underfoot; the gestures and regard of passing wildlife. This she did serenely, through countless hours of reflection. I imagine the process was rather like harvesting an orchard by hand, one fruit at a time. Though the orchard at the far end of the Hougoumont meadow has long since disappeared and I cannot prove this hypothesis.

Any details she couldn't glean or intuit she learned outright from visitors—the Eaton ladies, chiefly, who made a habit of lingering near the dovecote and sharing their reading. I must admit that I quaked a bit before those singular women, as I often did before Old Lavender herself, even if she happened to be my grandmother. Maybe it was their silver hair and unlined faces, a combination that is rare, I understand, and worthy of attention.

"Nature never truly recovers from human cataclysms," Grandmother said one day, to me alone. "Never." She was using *that* tone: two parts old sage, one part female warrior, scant affection and no salt. I suspected that she'd picked up some pointers listening to the Eaton ladies.

"Every creature who was anywhere near Waterloo sensed what was going to happen," she explained. "If they could, they got out. Those who stayed and survived passed the experience on through collective memory, right down through the generations until the present day. Collective memory . . . and resonance."

"Resonance?" I tried to give the word the same weight she had.

"Of course! Landscapes where great passion has been spilled resonate. Not loudly. But loud enough for most wild creatures to detect. Once set in motion, the vibrations continue forever."

Her look was grave. "Yes, William. *Forever.*" With a pinch of affection she added: "I'm telling you this because I believe you have my gift. We can all pick up vibrations. But you have the ability to interpret them, and pass them on. You should be aware of this now, even though you won't master your gift for many years. It's a responsibility, you know. Take great care with it."

3

A curious thing happened on nights of the full moon: Old Lavender would herd us summarily into the hutch even before Emmanuel stopped by and dismiss Spode from his lookout. Then she would linger outside in the run, as if she'd forgotten to reflect on something or other during the day and needed extra time in her hollow. If Emmanuel did turn up, he'd give his usual, cursory look for stragglers, but was often playing a game on his cell phone at the same time and frequently overlooked someone. Old Lavender he steered clear of. Even an oaf could summon the gray cells to fathom that this rabbit, always difficult, was unmanageable by the full moon.

Did you know there's a mythical rabbit in the moon? No? Well, there is one. You can trace its head, ears and tail in the various oceans on that heavenly body. Have a look, next time it's full. Some cultures think the animal is stirring something, or maybe pounding on a mortar. Others believe it is the Great Rabbit Himself—He who created the universe, that is. We were free to interpret the rabbit in the moon however we wished, though I've never reached a full understanding of the topic myself, being of modest intellect. But I like to think that since rabbits are generally seen at dawn and dusk, we act as gatekeepers of sorts for the night, and are somehow complicit in the rising and setting of our lunar relative. (This observation took quite a long time for me to formulate, by the way, and I'm rather proud of it.) There's little doubt that there *is* a rabbit in the moon. Now I just have to figure out what purpose he serves when he isn't rising or setting.

You may think the name of our god—Moon— rather unimaginative. Obvious, even. But you'd be wrong.

"There's *Moon*," Grandmother used to say.

"And there's *the* moon. Don't confuse them. Gods don't like to be tied down too much to their physical representations, and Moon is no exception. It smacks of idolatry, after all. The rabbit in the moon inspired the *idea* of our god (and the very tempting supposition that there is one at all). But Moon himself goes wherever he wants, whenever he wants. He's sometimes not even nearby when the moon is full. An ironic oversight, especially around here . . ."

We knew exactly what she was getting at. The Hougoumont night was not a normal phenomenon as nights go. How could it be, after what had happened there? The moon had only been a few days shy of full on the eighteenth of June, 1815, though the clouds were heavy and the moonlight unreliable. An insignificant detail, perhaps. Not many historians mention it. But if the full moon is anything, it's a handy lamp, and for the thousands who lay wounded on the Waterloo battlefield after sundown, their purgatory had only just begun. For the clouds would break from time to time, and when they did, the moon lit the plunderers' way.

Even the suggestion of plunderers made us head inside at night, which of course made Old Lavender's daily herding easier. It didn't matter that the threat was two hundred years old. She knew we had trouble distinguishing the centuries, and a plunderer was a plunderer, after all. What she wanted to impart was that twilight is a serious time for small animals. Foxes and owls lurk offstage, ever alert for a meal. Thus, strolling and stargazing were not encouraged in the colony (particularly with a lookout like Spode). Captivity tends to dull the senses, and we'd almost forgotten that predators existed at all. We'd grown complacent, I suppose. What better way to teach the dangers of the night, therefore, than with the dread of Napoleonic robbers—even if they hadn't been seen for some time?

I didn't mind going into the hutch during the full moon. The horde, the heat, the stench . . . such things seem normal, even agreeable, when you're young. It was just sad that no one was ever permitted to appreciate the spectacle of one of our own kind floating in the heavens. How we longed to defy the rule! Temptation sparred mightily with obedience, but eventually the conflict proved tiring, and we always straggled inside to bed.

"There a fine line between courage and recklessness," Old Lavender liked to point out. "One day, you may find yourself locked outside at night. You'll have to find that line very quickly; you'll have to summon your courage, then slowly rein it in, because otherwise you'll cross over to recklessness and end up as somebody's dinner."

She would cite the example of Marshal Ney for this lesson. Perhaps she admired him more than we thought. Though she labeled Ney "that spoiled hysteric," Old Lavender knew that he'd been dealt a bad hand at Quatre Bras.

The confrontation had occurred two days before the main battle at Waterloo and ended in a bloody stalemate of sorts. Ney's various orders had come late . . . or not at all. He'd found himself with too few troops to fight Wellington, and even fewer options. "Nothing was going right for Ney on June sixteenth, and history judged him harshly," Grandmother said. "When Napoleon sent him a message to hurry up, that was the last straw. Ney snapped. He crossed that line into recklessness, ordering an almost suicidal cavalry charge into Allied lines. He survived, though. So remember: If you find yourself shut out at night, think of the Marshal and his very bad day. If he could survive the British army, you have a pretty good chance of surviving one night out of doors."

∴

There was a rumor that Grandmother had escaped once.

Details were sketchy, but according to popular hearsay, one full moon several generations ago, she dug her way out of the enclosure and traversed the Untried, all the way to the eastern wall. No witnesses had ever come forward, and Old Lavender herself never spoke about it. So even though we lived next to the actual source of this legend, we might as well have been looking into a spring from which we were never permitted to drink.

I knew about it, though.

That is, I didn't see her escape, but I knew that she communed with something beyond the enclosure. I couldn't say how many times this had happened, or over how many years. I'd only defied her orders once, you see.

The moon was full that night—or nearly. Of that I'm certain, though on all other points my memory is a bit nebulous, because every second I spent outside I was frozen with alarm. Instinct seized my limbs. *Had Ney felt this way at Quatre Bras?* I wondered. And then: *How can I possibly be thinking about Marshal Ney at such a moment?* I couldn't have been bothered about the rabbit in the moon, although there he was, a whimsical gray squiggle on the surface of the glowing orb. Who cared if the squiggle was Moon himself? All I could think of was the darker gray of approaching wings.

I didn't see Old Lavender at first. She was in her usual hollow, which I hadn't expected, somehow. I'd assumed she would have chosen a safer spot: Jonas's earthworks under the hutch, for example. But there she was, upending all her own edicts, dallying under the full moon in a wide-open place. She was balancing on her hind legs in a stance I didn't even think she could manage anymore. Both ears were cocked forward. There was a wild, youthful aspect about her.

I shuffled up and stopped a few feet away. She would surely sense me at any moment, I remember thinking, as the wind was freshening behind me from the north. If so, I had to be ready to dart back into the hutch at once. Grandmother's punishment could be severe. These were just passing thoughts, however, insignificant before the greater pull I was experiencing: the wild impulse that played such havoc with the calm surface I was supposed to possess. Was this my gift kicking in? Surely not. The gift Grandmother had described was one of reflection, of intuition. Not this . . . not an urgent desire to leap over a fence.

Old Lavender was staring down the stretch of south wall. The moon had risen above the old beech: a harvest moon, overripe, expectant. Deep shadows cut across the silvery Untried. It seemed that light had shed its daytime duties and was doing whatever it fancied. It danced through the loopholes the British Guards had cut in the wall in 1815, and played unnervingly across the two bulbous tombstones of their fallen comrades, surfacing like mammals in a grassy sea. The memorial to the French rose like a buoy and threw a particularly frightening shadow. The monument had a cement eagle perched on top, and from it the moon had fashioned its black double on the grass.

The whole place was stage-lit, charged.

But inert.

Until something moved along the wall.

I peered where Old Lavender was peering: the movement skirted the tombs, vanished and then, to my horror, suddenly reappeared much closer, sidling slowly along the wall towards the pen. I knew that restless meadow well; I could only imagine that what I was witnessing was simply a manifestation of the usual rustling and sighing we heard each night.

But the thought rang false, somehow. Maybe I didn't know the meadow very well after all. The threat of Napoleonic plunderers didn't seem so far-fetched just then, and as the wind picked up, and the beech branch set up its tapping against the top of the wall, I found myself searching the rhythm for patterns, as if there might be some kind of signal in the sound.

Oddly, Old Lavender settled back onto all fours at that point, as if she'd found whatever it was she'd been looking for. Perhaps she'd deciphered a message of some sort, and was reassured that all was well.

The tapping ceased.

I could make out two distinctly denser patches against the wall now—one slender and taller; the other low-slung, pale. Old Lavender leaned toward them. Both forms swelled from the shadows, then melted away.

∴

Late November: dusk. I was daydreaming near the chicken wire before supper when Grandmother bumped against me rather heavily. "Don't you ever see them, William?" she asked, irritated.

What was she talking about?

"No" seemed the safest answer, so I said it.

"Well, don't you feel them, then? This is the perfect time of day for it."

"I . . . I don't think so." Then, weakly: "Who?"

My mind turned uneasily to the night of the full moon, and those shapes against the wall.

"Close your eyes," she snapped.

I did. But all I could think about was dinner. It was late, chilly, and I was too hungry for a lesson. The wind threw a clutch of dry leaves against the fence and befuddled me even further.

"You're not focusing," she said. *How did she know?* "That's better," she said. *Right again.*

She nosed my fur in the wrong direction, roughly. "Almost six thousand men died in this place on a single day."

I knew that already. Most of the time, any mention of the topic prompted much lurid banter in the colony. Jonas, in his element, would puff himself up and expound on the stacks of human corpses robbed of their clothes, and the communal fosse by the South Gate where they'd been dumped and burned. Why is it that the young always want to know about such things?

"Observe properly!" Grandmother hectored. "You may not be able to sense what I do without many more years of practice. But any novice can detect something unusual in the air around here."

She'd taught us the theory about that sort of observation. Perception is rarely immediate, she said. It takes time. First you must tune your senses:

You must slow all bodily and mental movement, and align your ears properly. And don't look at things from too close up. (If any creature needs reading glasses, it's rabbits.) It takes time to open up a space inside yourself wide enough to let ideas in and shed light on them.

Who could forget our first tutorial, when Old Lavender had us all stare up at the chapel spire for a whole hour?

"I told you several times what happened there," she said. "Weren't any of you listening? The wounded men were dragged inside the chapel; the fire licked through the door and singed only the feet of the crucifix. Then the flames suddenly retreated. *Why?* Open up your minds! Study the details. Be on the lookout for vibrations. The chapel was the site of great passion, after all. Was it the human god who saved it?" She paused to chew on some dry pellets. "Destiny?" With resignation she asked: "And what about our god? Would he have even arrived in time to put out the fire?"

Jonas managed about seven minutes of observation. Caillou needed to use the toilet after three. Spode, probably to impress his inamorata, continued for two hours, long after Old Lavender herself had called it a day and gone off to lunch. For my part, I hung on for a good half an hour, after which my haunches began to quiver with that familiar restiveness and I moved off to study the meadow.

There was something about Grandmother's tone now, as the keen November wind came off the fields, that made me feel as if I were learning the observation lesson all over again.

She ruffled my fur sternly. "Listen for the traffic of souls, William." There was an uncharacteristic, pleading note in her voice. "There are enough of them around to leave a faint heaviness on the air, like dew. Surely you, of all my kin, must feel it. They're quite spacious, those fields. But that's still quite a lot of traffic."

"Can you see them, Grandmother?"

"Sometimes. Through that breach in the eastern wall." She indicated the tumbled-down bricks at the far end of the meadow. *Was that what she looked at when the moon was full?*

I was quite familiar with that breach. In dreamy moments, I occasionally imagined the Duke of Wellington riding by it on his way through the orchard.

"Guilt keeps them from settling," she went on. "They care far less about *being* killed than they do about *having* killed."

How she knew this, I can't tell you. But she

would say things like that and then not speak for three days. All sorts of disturbances moved into her silence then—unidentified things, of the sort one didn't want to contemplate when the shadows lengthened along the south wall.

∴

Emmanuel hadn't the wits to look after us properly, he was too old for school, and he was certainly too fat to ride a bicycle. But he was obliged to do one or another of these things occasionally, and it was on the morning he had to do all three that the lapse occurred.

We weren't sure what to make of the open gate at first.

We were suddenly, suspiciously, free. The gate lolled in the wind and let out a mournful sigh, as it always did when open. But it was strange: after the initial incredulity, we weren't very happy about this state of affairs. It's often like that, isn't it? You want something so badly that you can think of nothing else; you lust after it selfishly, and daydream about it, and indulge the idea at odd hours until you're only half engaged with the world around you. The want turns to obsession, and the obsession leaves you exhausted. Then the miracle happens: you get what you wanted. But after all that, you wonder why it isn't quite what you'd had in mind.

All I can say is that on that October morning, with the mist curling like winding sheets through the ancient Hougoumont trees, I caught my first glimpse of Moon and didn't much like what I saw.

We all milled uncertainly in the opening that had once been a gate—that now, oddly, looked incomplete, as if the gate really should have been there. We could still hear the clatter of Emmanuel's bicycle fading away down the lane. Clearly he thought that he'd finished for the day and would not be coming back.

"Freedom is not always what it's made out to be," Old Lavender liked to say, perhaps to make our lifelong incarceration less onerous. "It may be a good thing in the abstract, but on the ground, someone always ends up paying for it."

Little did we know that her words were about to be put to the test. Surely I wasn't the only one recalling her standard admonitory triplet: "Look up! Use your nose! Make connections!" (*Especially when things don't seem right*, she often added.) I do remember that in all the confusion at the open gate, quite a few of us were looking up, noses twitching at twice the normal speed, trying desperately to make connections. Something, after all, was far from right.

Perhaps the oddest thing about that moment of dubious liberty was that Old Lavender herself was nowhere to be seen. She'd retired to the hutch—something that only nursing mothers or the sick did during the day. Another one of her cryptic signals, I thought later . . . one that I should have been able to read.

We operated through brainless instinct from that point onward. In a rush of impulse—and probably to impress Jonas—I ventured out of the gate first. Jonas followed at my heels. It was as if William of Orange and Marshal Ney were going nose-to-tail on some historical nightmare of a mission.

Unquestioning, everyone filed after us, Caillou in the rear. We crept along the interior wall of the compound to the barred gate through which cows passed back and forth between barns and meadow. Even then, the farm was subsiding into ruin. The bricks of the wall bulged with soft, mossy tumors. We had to flatten ourselves to traverse a grotesque tangle of fading, sky-high nettle and prickly vines. Ivy choked every available pasage.

We made it through this jungle and slipped easily under the cow barrier.

Suddenly there we were, in the scarred heart of Hougoumont.

The magnitude of it must have struck us all simultaneously, for once we'd skirted the little chapel, we all stopped together in a tight huddle, spellbound. It was as if a host of bedtime stories had come disturbingly alive. History itself seemed to reach down with a cool hand. There, ahead of us, was the great barn with its open porch; to the right, the track leading to the infamous North Gate; on our left, the gardener's house, shuttered and inscrutable. Under our feet, cobblestones whirled in ancient patterns. Grass and moss had pushed between them and turned most of the courtyard into a dreamy wash of green. Someone had left a wreath of poppies against the wall of the chapel. Aside from this crimson tingle of life, there was no movement, no sound. Even death, having once gorged here, seemed absent.

Caillou broke the silence: "Is that the barn where they took the French drummer boy?"

"They probably took him into the chateau for safety," Spode sniffed, ever the professor.

"I thought the chateau was in flames," Jonas challenged.

"That was later . . . " Spode waffled.

"Where did he come from?" Caillou asked. "What was his name?"

"No one knows," Spode said.

"I don't like it here," moaned Berthe, trembling violently.

We were all speaking in a hush, as the atmosphere pressed heavily and seemed to demand it. There was no wind in the courtyard, the autumn mist just a gauzy thickening in the air. Perhaps it was fitting that Old Lavender should come to mind at that moment, curiously absent though she was from this madcap adventure. *A place of great conflict should bring on great reflection. If it doesn't, all might as well have happened in vain.* I'm not sure if Grandmother's words had entered the others' heads, but they were certainly echoing in mine, and it did seem a sacrilege, somehow, not to pause in the middle of that courtyard and honor the blood that had been spilled there.

We all took a moment. But only one, mind you, as no rabbit can ever feel safe in an open space.

The Eaton ladies always idled in the courtyard whenever they visited. They sometimes murmured the words of their mentor, Charlotte Eaton, who herself had visited Hougoumont just a month after the battle:

"The *château* itself, the beautiful seat of a Belgic gentleman, had been set on fire by the explosion of shells during the action, which had completed the destruction occasioned by a most furious cannonade. Its broken walls and falling roof presented a most melancholy spectacle . . . its huge blackened beams had fallen in every direction upon the crumbling heaps of stone and plaster, which were intermixed with broken pieces of the marble flags, the carved cornices, and the gilded mirrors that once ornamented it."

(All this may seem like a lot of mental activity for a single moment, but it's amazing what the brain can do under pressure.)

The moment, however, was past. No historical importance could detain us any longer. We broke our huddle and filed past the gardener's house to the South Gate. Arriving there occasioned another, astonished halt: that gate, too, was open! Had Emmanuel sunk to a new, delinquent low? Was the farmer ill? Uncertain, we skittered over the cobbles and massed beneath a stone archway.

The stone archway! I thrilled. This must be where Private Matthew Clay had come across the drummer boy! The thought gave a satisfying crack, like a tough seed, though the tasty historical kernel soon vanished, and plain old terror took its place.

Caillou stepped out first. Not because of any superior boldness, of course, but because, as the runt of the colony, he'd been caught up in the mass of swirling fur and jettisoned out the other side like the pebble after which he'd been named. *How could Old Lavender have known to call him what she did?* The creature was now bolting toward the fallow field behind the chestnuts. With inappropriate whimsy, I wondered whether Grandmother had predicted all along that this fateful day would come, and in anticipation named Caillou after the headquarters Napoleon had set up on the day before his downfall.

We stared after the runt, too terrified to even utter his name. He'd scaled the ditch at the edge of the field now, and was advancing in pitiful, jerky leaps across the vast Untried. His pale gray coat would have been visible for miles.

Was I the first to notice the hawk? I don't remember. As instructed by Old Lavender, I was obediently looking up, even though everyone else was disobeying her and tracking the progress of poor Caillou. So yes, I probably was the first to spot the hunched form at the top of one of the chestnuts.

Allow me to pause here for the sake of those trees.

Those trees . . .

Witnesses, judges, confessors. Call them what you will, but they cannot be ignored.

The principal gates of Hougoumont are on the north and south sides of the farm. The first French assault came from the south, through woods that are now gone. Three tortured chestnuts are the only remaining trees from that forest and stand just across the courtyard from the South Gate. Two of the them, in death, seem to have hardened into wax effigies. Barkless, they are as pale as the naked corpses that were thrown into the pit at their feet. They resemble thick-bottomed obelisks, their trunks tapering at the top, and they are monumental to behold.

The third chestnut is alive—though barely, as if through the fumbling intervention of somebody's god. In autumn, its leaves become mottled like the hands of an old farmer, and chestnuts hang in valiant clusters, undersized and sickly. But like its fellows, this tree bears the scars of deep wounds and has its own, lifeless crest. It seems to be slowly, eloquently dying from the top down.

The living chestnut is plainly visible from the South Gate, so we could see perfectly well that on its summit, stenciled against the sky, sat an agent of death.

We could also still see Caillou—those of us not

preoccupied with matters in the tree, that is. He was tripping over the deep ruts in the field now, panic having entirely supplanted any trace of rational thought—of instinct, even. That instinct should have warned him to flatten himself against the earth; or at least reminded him to be on the lookout for any nearby rabbit warren and dart down it. I found myself eyeing not only the hawk, but the milky sky behind him, wondering whether Moon might make an appearance at some point, this being an opportune moment.

The hawk seemed in no hurry. He floated languorously down from his perch with a soft *thurrup* of wings, as if he weren't an exquisitely tuned hunting machine at all, but just a pigeon on its beat, coming in to check for stray seeds.

There was a single, terrifying screech . . . the sort of sound that haunts you for the rest of your days.

The milling in the archway froze, as if a wand had passed overhead. Defying all instinct, I pushed my way out of the huddle in time to see the hawk rise up high over the south wall. He was slowed by his burden, and I could just make out a flaccid, pale gray object hanging from his talons before the mist swallowed them both, fur and feather alike.

We remained in tight formation for some time. It struck me later that we must have resembled one of those squares Wellington's troops adopted in the thick of battle. Such formations never seemed very fair to those on the outside of the square, in my opinion, which was where I happened to find myself at that moment, though Old Lavender had assured me, during one of my Waterloo lessons, that Wellington's squares had been very effective for stopping cavalry charges. Which wasn't much comfort when facing a hawk, mind you, but one had to forgive Old Lavender for not being versed in all aspects of battle formation.

I peered out at the belly of mist that had swallowed Caillou and his destiny. Almost immediately, the mist began to come apart and drift away over the fields, as if it had accomplished its role as one of the dramatis personae and was heading for intermission. I tracked the wisps of ghostly air, hoping for a glimpse of that enigmatic fellow Old Lavender had mentioned so many times. But Moon, if he'd come at all, had left quickly. It was tempting to imagine that he had slipped in invisibly, taken Caillou by the paw and led him gently away, as Grandmother said he did when someone died. But now we knew for a fact that that wasn't true. Two dozen of us had been looking up, after all; we'd seen exactly what had happened. Perhaps

Moon had suddenly taken on the guise of a hawk, and Caillou's terrible shriek had been one of trans-figuration, not anguish. But that would have made for some complicated scripture, and such matters are complicated enough.

A musket ball to the ribs; a hawk swooping in . . . death comes in an infinite array of disguises. But once arrived, its face is always the same—or so it seems to me. I'd seen enough inert lumps of fur pushed against the fence, and smelled that peculiar gaminess in the hutch to know when death had stopped by. I didn't actually see Caillou after he'd died, it's true. But I feel sure that even he, so quickly reduced to a meal, would have briefly taken on that aura everyone does at some point—a magnetic stillness more powerful than loss, or grief, or even love: the handprint of rapturous homecoming.

There wasn't a moment to lose. We headed back to the enclosure posthaste, scrabbling over the slippery cobbles, making evasive leaps in case there were other hawks in the vicinity who had heard about the fine dining at Hougoumont. We slunk back through the open gate and filed directly into the hutch—unusually, as it was only midday. Emmanuel wouldn't be back again for another day or two, depending on whether or not he remembered having come that morning, and the farmer rarely checked in on us. That meant that the gate of the enclosure would remain open all night.

Old Lavender greeted us curtly, then resumed a stony silence in her own reserved corner of the hutch. No one uttered Caillou's name—it didn't seem necessary, somehow. Old Lavender seemed to know already what had happened; I'm sure she'd known for some time that the runt was doomed. No one uttered my name, either, thank heavens, although Grandmother would find out soon enough who had led the excursion.

When she emerged the next day, she went directly to the hollow and immersed herself in reflection. Her ears assumed their customary, skewed position. But her aspect was more forbidding, somehow. Warily, I settled against the earth a bit farther from her than usual. Had yesterday's disaster prompted thoughts of her own legendary escape? I wondered. My imagination raced. I couldn't help speculating that Grandmother's escapade, festering off-limits in colony lore, had left something unfinished at the core of her being that continued to work on her day and night. Our disaster had clearly added to the burden. Her silence was weighted with all the lessons she

had taught us, as obviously as if she had hung a
reminder on the chicken wire. Indeed, we seemed
to be amply punished just by her mute, smelly
displeasure.

It actually wasn't so bad, nestling against my
own piece of earth for a change. It gave me a
chance to come to my own conclusions about yesterday, as unformed as they may have been at my
young age. I'm not sure if I was recalling something
Grandmother had once told us, or if I had actually
come up with this myself, but I realized, after our
abortive escape, that there's an optimal time for
everything. Casting a furtive glance at Old Lavender, I considered that if she had indeed slipped out
herself once, she may have chosen the wrong time,
and that's why she'd come back. Patience is the key.
To do something important at the wrong moment
is worse than not doing it at all.

I should have avoided that open gate. The
moment had been about as wrong as could be.

I shifted in the dirt. I'd acted mindlessly, stepping out even before Jonas on an adventure that
had ended in death. Now I saw how fitting it had
been to name me after the naïve Prince of Orange.
Not everyone called his actions "heroic determination," as Napoleon had. Some accounts show that
the Prince had brought destruction to a company

of men at Quatre Bras through a deadly mix of impulse and inexperience.

I didn't have as many deaths on my conscience as William of Orange, perhaps. But I had Caillou's. And at that moment, I was sure that no regret, princely or otherwise, could have matched my own.

My heart ached for the poor runt. I longed for Grandmother to shed some light on what had happened that morning at the South Gate. I mean, think about it: Is a single death—especially the death of a creature that the human species considers insignificant enough to eat—of any universal importance at all in a place where thousands of men have died? (Or in any other place, for that matter?) For the human animal, probably not. But for us . . . for us . . . . Oh, can you not step outside the human mind-set for just a moment and imagine the remorse I felt?

I studied Old Lavender as she sat alone in our hollow, and began to understand that she wanted me to sort these things out for myself.

That was the day I grew up.

4

Jonas may have been the finest physical spec-
imen of our colony, but I do think (not to be
immodest about it) that I was one of the better
students. I had the privilege of a higher education,
after all, sharing that hollow with our grandmother;
and like her, I was also a secret admirer of the
Eaton ladies. I tarried at the fence during their vis-
its, tracking each step of their progress around the
meadow. Whenever they rested near the dovecote
and Old Lavender drew near them, I was never far
behind her. I'm sure that the snow-and-moon ladies

never dreamed that their reading aloud so close to the Hougoumont rabbit enclosure would be sifted and analyzed by the long-eared matriarch behind the fence, and eagerly stored away by her young apostle.

Charlotte Eaton herself traveled to Brussels from Ghent on June 15, 1815, accompanied by her brother and sister, and taking the same road along which Napoleon Bonaparte had made his triumphant progress some twenty years before. The French surrendered this territory in 1814—known officially at the time as "the Austrian (Southern) Netherlands"—but Napoleon, of course, would make one more attempt to conquer it at Waterloo.

As her carriage advanced down the tree-lined *chaussée* and stopped at inns and hamlets along the way, Charlotte encountered a universal hatred and fear of the former rulers, an emotion that burst forth from villagers spontaneously, "as if they could not suppress it; their whole countenances change; their eyes sparkle with indignation; they seem at a loss for words strong enough to express the bitterness of their detestation." This lingering spite notwithstanding, the countryside wore the appearance of plenty—of hope, even. Verdant farms, neat cottages and luxuriant corn all signaled prosperity. Barefoot children ran, laughing, behind the carriage and offered flowers. As Charlotte began her journey southward, she naïvely thought that peace was at hand.

She soon perceived her error.

In the hot, sultry air of that June two hundred years ago, events were moving behind the scenes with dark swiftness. Charlotte Eaton was perhaps not the most gifted air-reader, it must be said. But if she had studied the details of those days as Old Lavender would have (a Thursday through Sunday, I believe they were)—had perceived the swollen foreboding in them—she would have clearly noticed that Nature was gathering fear and dread to her bosom. The air, forest, soil and all their occupants sensed that human cataclysm was nigh. Even if the natural world wasn't quite sure when or where, exactly, war was about to break out again, or even that it was Bonaparte himself who happened to be breathing at the door (all human tyrants are alike, after all), a warning had been sounded. Horses and cattle shifted and twitched; small creatures burrowed deep, waiting. The weather brooded, gathered itself and at times broke in brief, violent premonition.

By the time the Eaton party had arrived in Brussels, the entire city was wearing a military aspect. But how well the magnificence of a soldier masks his job! Charlotte marveled at the tassels and epaulets, the clasps and crosses and braids . . . not things that, when seen on a fine young man, one could ever imagine being darkened with his blood, or left behind in the dirt after he's been thrown into a communal grave. One didn't have to imagine it . . . at least, not yet.

The Eatons entered a city brimming with fine young men. Despite all the rumors charging the air, there was a vigor to the outpost that proved irresistible. The thronged streets pulsed with confidence and expectation, as if something important were about to happen, but to someone else, and not anytime soon. Allied soldiers in every variety of uniform mingled with the locals in convivial groups, or took a turn with the ladies down one of the shaded avenues of the Parc de Bruxelles. There were English soldiers in their red coats and white belts, and hearty, laughing Highlanders, as renowned in battle for their fierceness as for those unimpeachable kilts. Only the so-called Black Brunswickers, a corps under the command of the amiable Duke of Brunswick and kept in reserve by Wellington, offered a bleak counterpoint. They dressed in black, and rode black horses. On their heads they wore shakos decorated with sinister death's heads and plumes of black horsehair. Their long, regular procession looked "like an immense moving hearse," Charlotte noted, "that one might take for a bad omen."

Twilight drifted in on the humid haze. Dispatches flew from servant to officer, hotelier to guest, washerwoman to valet. *The fighting has begun! But how far off do you suppose it is? Are the French in great number? Where are the Prussians?* There was no reliable intelligence anywhere. The mood in Brussels traced a great, emotive arc: from the depths of French-fueled panic, to the heights of incredulous relief, and back down to the French again.

Daylight lingered, as it does during a northern June.

Night fell.

After they had dined, officers donned their stockings and dancing shoes. For the Duchess of Richmond's ball was going ahead as planned.

∴

Now, I would like to reduce the stage of events a bit, if I may—well, quite a lot, actually. Specifically, to the size of our hutch. For it was there, in the pleasant fug of dozing family members, that Old Lavender occasionally took us to the Duchess of Richmond's ball.

Grandmother wasn't much of a sentimentalist, as you've probably gathered by now, her prefer-

ence leaning more towards military strategy—
battle formations, cavalry charges and the like. So
it wasn't often that she told us this story. I suspect
that she had to force the dreamy tone she used for
the ball scene—not an easy feat for such a hard-
boiled old rabbit. Her efforts succeeded, however,
for I had only to close my eyes to step easily into
that long, low-ceilinged room.

The Duke of Richmond had rented the space
in Rue de la Blanchisserie from his neighbor in
Brussels, a coach builder. Richmond himself was
in charge of a reserve force to protect Brussels in
case of a surprise invasion by Napoleon. Bonaparte was a wily adversary, after all. One never
knew with him. But despite conflicting reports of
his movements, it was thought that the emperor
was still quite a way off, and under the circumstances, perhaps a bit of merrymaking might keep
fate from the door for a few more hours.

In retrospect, the ball was a gathering of but-
terflies at the foot of a smoking volcano.

The "volcano" was Quatre Bras: the crossroads south of Waterloo that would turn out to be
the prelude to full-scale eruption. I'd heard about
those crossroads. Old Lavender always mentioned
them whenever she talked about the ball, so we
wouldn't forget that war had been biding its time.

Just out there, she would say, indicating the door of the hutch. *Just outside the Richmonds' window.*

Quatre Bras used to be an obscure country intersection (literal meaning: "four arms"). Towering corn, dense woodland and only four gabled cottages, shut and alert, marked the spot. Everything shimmered in a mirage of heat. And the stillness . . . not of bucolic peace, but that other kind . . . the kind that presages an earthquake, or a tempest. No creature could have ignored it.

"Oh, the animals knew what was about to happen," Grandmother said. "Those who could, fled. The others . . ." She paused dramatically. "The others could only pull into their shells for protection, or crawl down to their deepest chambers. Remember your Thomas Hardy!"

And we did—well, most of us only remembered the part about the fleeing coneys. But I had memorized the rest of Hardy's Waterloo poem, and even whispered it aloud now and then, just to honor our doomed neighbors, though invariably I had to stop after the worm, sick-hearted:

> . . . *The worm asks what can be overhead,*
> *And wriggles deep from a scene so grim,*
> *And guesses him safe; for he does not know*
> *What a foul red flood will be soaking him!* . . .

The Richmonds' dancing and dining went on until the early hours. How well Old Lavender described it, her military preferences notwithstanding! So well that I can hear the music even now: the jaunty dances and gliding tunes; the genteel stomping on parquet floors. I can smell the warm, humid air, too, thick with perfume and the mushroomy promise of dinner (not necessarily rabbit, we were assured). The low room was decorated with rose-trellised wallpaper, and rich draperies of crimson, gold and black. Pillars were wreathed in ribbons and flowers. They danced reels and cotillions. The list of beauty and chivalry glittered. Handsome lads in uniform took care with their grips, accustomed as they were to gun barrels and not the feminine upper arm. The Prince of Orange and Duke of Wellington were themselves guests, but only in passing, as they were just hours away from the first salvos of battle. No one could describe it better than Grandmother:

> On with the dance! let joy be unconfined; . . .
> . . . But hark!—that heavy sound breaks in once more,
> As if the clouds its echo would repeat;
> And nearer, clearer, deadlier than before;
> Arm! arm! it is—it is—the cannon's opening roar!

Some of you may have noticed that these are not, in fact, the words of Old Lavender, but those of Lord Byron, though one can hardly blame her for overlooking such a thing in the heat of storytelling. For our part, we couldn't have cared less. By the time Old Lavender was quoting Byron, we had long since left the hutch for the ball.

The evening's most eminent guests would miss their supper, alas. At around ten, a dispatch arrived for the Prince of Orange from Quatre Bras, announcing that the French had repulsed the Prussians northeast of Charleroi, a surprising skirmish, and far nearer than expected. The Prince slipped away from the party at once; Wellington continued to smile politely for another twenty minutes or so before slipping out himself.

A bugle sounded on the Place Royale before dawn, and then another: the unmistakable call to arms. Drums instantly set up their beating. Bagpipes blared the pibroch—the Highland martial summons. The commotion woke Charlotte Eaton and her sister in their hotel room overlooking the *place*. (They had not been invited to the ball.) They gazed out at the tumult and confusion of arms clanging, orders shouted, wagons rolling heavily by. Women could even be seen mounting their horses to follow their husbands into battle.

At the Richmonds', officers were asked to leave the ball quietly and rejoin their units. Soldiers hastened into the night, shuffling and unsure. They turned back to their loved ones many times, unable as they were to face the last, inevitable turn back. Musket butts rang on the cobbles. Chargers neighed and skittered over the slick stones, the clatter punctuated by loud, deep-toned commands. Some soldiers were still wearing their silk stockings and dancing pumps as they marched off to fight.

Quite a few would never go dancing again.

⁘

Many conflicting accounts have been written about Quatre Bras.

"In my opinion" (Grandmother always ended her ball story with this comment), "it was Prince William of Orange who took the initiative and held off the French until reinforcements arrived. He doesn't get enough credit, I don't think. He made some ill-considered decisions on the battlefield, it's true. He was only twenty-three, after all. But he had guts, that boy. Napoleon said as much himself, during one of his many idle moments on St. Helena."

I knew that Grandmother considered the Prince

a foolish lad in many ways. But she also called him brave and impulsive, and that comment more than made up for any slight implied by naming me after him. She also said: "Nothing is worse than knowing you might have done something and didn't."

She insisted that Wellington had gone to the ball uneasily, just to maintain public morale. *It was not a carefree affair, William.*

Indeed.

But I never paid much attention whenever Old Lavender tried to dampen my pleasure in the ball. I just couldn't repress that image of the Duke, gazing mistily at the trellised wallpaper, his heart softening to some lady or other while of course in reality, as he was politely nodding and smiling at the ladies, he was busy evaluating, strategizing, galvanizing and postulating, among many other activities of four syllables or more with which inferior men have scant acquaintance.

When news reached the ball that Napoleon had crossed the frontier, Wellington and Richmond ducked into the latter's dressing room.

"Napoleon has humbugged me, by God!" Wellington declared. "He has gained twenty-four hours' march on me."

The two men pored over a map. Wellington placed his thumbnail on a small village nine miles south of Brussels: Waterloo. "If we will not stop him at Quatre Bras, I must fight him here."

You can see how, as a young romantic, I preferred a mistier version of the ball.

∴

I never much cared who won or lost, or who said what to whom, whenever I went to the Richmonds'. I never had trouble finding that soft, redolent, richly hued space in my head. Perhaps it was the proximity of family before falling asleep—the muffle of fur and gamey humidity that, together with Grandmother's soothing drone, somehow metamorphosed the hutch into a more exalted setting. Even now, when I have trouble falling asleep, I drift off to that splendid ballroom. I imagine the tap of dancing shoes against the wooden floor; the whoosh of silk; the murmuring elegance. And always, before sleep overtakes me, I can see the red-coated Arthur Wellesley, first Duke of Wellington, taking a turn around the floor, his face set with deeper concerns. His boots made no sound, of course. He was above that sort of thing. He wasn't entirely in focus, either, but shimmered hazily, like the early autumn mists at the far end of the meadow. His high embroidered collar kept his chin aloft, and the golden braid over his shoulder swung as he moved. And in his eyes, the cool, even shine of duty . . .

"You mustn't idolize Wellington too much, William." No one could spoil a good reverie like Grandmother. "There's nothing more boring than a fairy-tale hero. Did you know that his mother described him as 'awkward,' and that he was an unremarkable student? He could be cold, aloof, controlling. And I bet you didn't know that his soldiers called him 'Old Nosey' on account of that prominent feature of his."

I wasn't sure what she was getting at with all this. I'd never met anyone as cold, aloof and controlling as Old Lavender could be, though I loved her dearly. We all have our faults, don't we? Maybe those "boring" heroes, so irritatingly glorious, have a special role to play in making up for all of our own shortcomings, even if in reality their exploits are far from perfect.

I rarely countered my grandmother to her face, on this or any other subject. But I must confess that Wellington's indifferent school performance, his coldness, his prominent nose . . . none of it tarnished the strapping, broad-shouldered Duke who glided across my imagination, and whom I would have happily called "Old Nosey" had I been fortunate enough to be born in his era, as something other than what I was, wearing a red uniform.

⸪

The fighting at Quatre Bras was so fierce that it could be heard in Brussels, almost eighty kilometers away. The cannonade continued unabated throughout the day of June 16, filling the population with terror and suspense. No one could be sure what was happening at the front. Rumors confirmed the worst—that the French would soon invade the town—only to be contradicted by stragglers from the battlefield, or citizens coming to their own, random conclusions.

On street corners, in shops, at pâtisseries and cafés, residents clapped their cheeks in despair. *The Belgians have abandoned their arms and fled! The French are advancing on Brussels*, nom de Dieu! Scuffles erupted on city squares. *Idiot, what are you saying? That old rascal Blücher has given the French a thrashing!*

Nothing, and no one, could be believed.

People rushed home to gather their possessions for flight. The Parc de Bruxelles, so recently the scene of splendid uniforms and strolling ladies, was deserted. Charlotte Eaton wandered its paths and lingered on the city's boulevards and squares, hoping for news. By the end of the day, it seemed as if the cannons were growing ever louder and nearer. Towards nine in the evening, there was one tremendous, final burst, and at length the sound diminished and faded away.

What fine use Charlotte could have made of a lagomorph's intuition that day! Without it— without being able to discern the exact nature and location of hostilities, or evaluate the depth of anxiety and deception revealed through voice and body language, there was only one sensible thing to do: flee.

Every creature who was anywhere near Waterloo sensed what was going to happen. If they could, they got out . . .

Charlotte Eaton was no Old Lavender. But she knew, even without an accurate reading of the air, that it would have been madness to stay in Brussels any longer.

By the time she and her party had come to this conclusion, however, a stampede was heading for the exits. Not a single horse was available anywhere. Carriages were seized by force. On every corner, a frantic babble of languages lamented, squabbled, exclaimed, implored. No one doubted that evil lurked just outside the city limits, wearing a French uniform. The very idea threatened to

shred public order entirely, though as the wagon-
loads of dead and wounded began to trickle into
Brussels, many stoic hearts stayed behind to help.

At the Eatons' Hôtel de Flandre on the Place
Royale, rooms were abandoned in haste, their
doors gaping open, candles still burning inside.
Below, noted Charlotte, the mistress of the hotel,
"with a countenance dressed in woe, was carrying
off her most valuable plate in order to secure it,
ejaculating, as she went, the name of Jesus inces-
santly, and, I believe, unconsciously; while the
master, with a red nightcap on his head, and the
eternal pipe sticking mechanically out of one corner of his mouth, was standing with his hands in
his pockets, a silent statue of despair."

The first wounded stragglers appeared: Prussians and Belgians, each man bearing his own
unique horror written in dirt and blood. For a soldier, the sight was as ordinary as a slaughtered ox
to a farmer.

But not for an English lady.

"The moment in which I first saw some of these
unfortunate people was, I think, one of the most
painful I ever experienced," Charlotte wrote, "and
soon, very soon, they arrived in numbers. At every
jolt of the slow wagons upon the rough pavement

we seemed to feel the excruciating pain which they must suffer."

The Eatons eventually secured a carriage, and on June 17 they became refugees along with thousands of others. Slowly, haltingly, they made their way to Antwerp, where they had a better chance of finding a boat back to England if things should come to that.

The day was sultry, the journey oppressive and fraught. Grim-faced, each traveler silently bore the weight of the reality unfolding just a few kilometers away, where the wounded lay helpless on the battlefield in the same, blazing heat, without shelter or water. Ladies whose lives had centered on drawing room comforts confronted horrors that would change them forever. For weeks, war to them had just been lively, colorful words. Now they knew the truth: that no civilized language could describe what was happening within earshot.

The amiable Duke of Brunswick was one of the first casualties of Quatre Bras.

The hearty, laughing Highlanders were felled almost to a man.

A stream of misery flooded Antwerp, clogging all available hospitals, hotels, private lodgings, hovels and tents. Wounded soldiers were billeted with ordinary citizens. Those without such luxury languished on doorsteps, under bridges, on open squares. Countless others, abandoned by providence, expired in the backs of the wagons that had dragged them from the field.

French soldiers were among the casualties, and were cared for like the rest. Indeed, war's perverse logic began to filter through the horror, and little by little, inhumanity revealed itself, until the sight of it, naked, overpowered the hate and suspicion that had caused it in the first place.

Society loosened its guard on all fronts.

"At this momentous crisis, one feeling actuated every heart—one thought engaged every tongue—one common interest bound together every human being. All ranks were confounded; all distinctions leveled; British and foreigners were all upon an equality . . ."

The Eatons found lodging in the same hotel in which the corpse of the Duke of Brunswick occupied a room. The body had already been embalmed, and all evening and well into the night, members of the British and foreign military filed in to pay their respects.

It was past midnight when Charlotte found herself sitting alone, listening to the rain resume with all its former intensity. Through the deluge, other sounds could be distinguished, of alarm filling the streets, and carriages rattling past, and refugees beating on doors in vain attempts to find shelter.

At length the clamor settled, and the downpour muffled the night.

Sometime before dawn, a sharp tapping punctured the stillness: someone was nailing down the coffin of the Duke of Brunswick.

The next morning, the square outside the hotel sprouted with umbrellas as people gathered for news.

It was Sunday, June 18, 1815.

5

One muggy afternoon in June, I was leaning against the chicken wire without a thought in my head when Old Lavender opened a narrow slit of eye.

"You'll be leaving here soon," she said.

The comment smacked me unawares, like a falling chestnut.

The sound of her voice was hollow and slightly menacing. I inched away, momentarily stunned by this message from the oracle.

"But I'll come back someday, won't I?" I
ventured.

"No," she said.

"Never?"

Old Lavender went back to her thinking. Distant thunder stalked the fields and the air grew
heavier.

"Never," she said at last. Her truths always shut
cleanly, like the door of a well-made hutch.

Of course I knew I would never come back. No
one ever did. Why should I be any different?

I watched a magpie skitter down over the top of
the wall and begin a jaunty walk along the perimeter of the enclosure. He pecked casually, eyeing
us as he went. There was something opportunistic
about his gait and I shivered, remembering what
Old Lavender had said about the crowds that visited the field of Waterloo on the day after the battle. Some were looking for loved ones, of course.
But others were simply out to rob the corpses.

"Why do you fight the truth so?" she asked,
grinding her teeth on a troublesome corn kernel.
"It could be your ally, if only you would let it."

"How do I let it?"

But she'd dozed off. A few minutes later she
resurfaced and said: "Accept it, for one thing."

"But I don't want to leave Hougoumont!" I cried. I pushed against the fence again and stared out at the meadow with entirely new eyes. The idea of imminent departure made me feel ill. *How could I leave here?*

"You will not be leaving alone."

Hope surged. "Who's coming with me?" I asked. The thought of having company, even if it meant being crammed into a crate with relatives, and that some of us would end up at the abattoir, opened a window onto this catastrophe.

"That's not what I was getting at," Old Lavender bristled. She seemed quite unmoved by the prospect of my leaving. "What I meant was: you will be taking your gift with you—*my* gift, which will assure you a lifetime of illumination, no matter where you end up. That, and . . . "

"And?" I was hoping she would come up with something more promising than the gift of picking up errant signals.

"And Hougoumont, of course."

"Hougoumont?" As if in answer, the humid air stirred and the beech branch gave a faint tap on the wall. In a moment of anguish I thought of Caillou, and how much he had loved the story about the French drummer boy.

Stillness fell again, trailed by a long roll of thunder. A few fat raindrops slapped against the dry earth in the pen.

"Hougoumont is at your core, William. Like a power source. All homes, physical or ephemeral, work that way."

∴

Old Lavender had certainly read the air correctly, for it was just as she had predicted— only much sooner than I could ever have imagined. The next morning, Emmanuel came at dawn and loaded me into a banana crate along with a large selection of cousins.

I just wish that Spode hadn't sought me out before the boy scooped me up.

Emmanuel dropped the crate with a significance that sent me leaping pell-mell into every corner to find Old Lavender. *How could I leave without saying good-bye?* Rain was pulsing in billows from the north now, cloaking the wizard trees and deepening their torpor. You would never have known that the moon had been close to full the night before. "Peculiarly awful" was how Grandmother had described the storm on the eve of Waterloo, and as I understand it, the weather hadn't improved much by the next morning. So here I was, I thought, at the dawn of my own Waterloo, if not as petrified as the men who had waited all night for battle, at least as wet.

I paid a final visit to the hollow: Grandmother wasn't there. Anyway, our spot—the cherished site of my awakenings—had been transformed into a small lake. I poked my head into the hutch: perhaps I shouldn't have, because doing so only confirmed without a doubt that Old Lavender was gone, and destroyed my last remaining hope of nourishing myself for the rest of my life on thoughts of her, resplendent at the center of the colony, the planet around which we all revolved.

Spode materialized from the mist. "Old Lavender disappeared last night, William," he said, deeply shaken.

I could barely breathe. His comment cemented all my fears. A frenzied spinning gripped my mind: images of foxes and owls tumbled together with Napoleonic plunderers and even with Emmanuel, poor fellow, who in my panic had morphed into a villain and opportunist (unfair, I suppose, but I knew so few people).

"But how?" I gasped.

Spode said nothing. He nudged me into the hutch out of the rain.

Something in my devastation must have brought a whole new facet to light in Spode, for his normally chilly demeanor warmed up. In the next few minutes, he would say more to me than he had in the three years I'd lived in the colony.

"I promised your grandmother I wouldn't breathe a word of what happened last night, William. So you must respect that."

"So you know!"

He ignored me and said: "As you will be leaving soon, perhaps you should know about the other time that she . . . well . . . *slipped out.*"

"The other time?" I echoed.

Spode nodded. "The last time was many years ago, long before you were born. The moon was just a few days shy of full—like last night. But the evening long ago was clear, fresh. Your grandmother was lingering outside alone, as she liked to do on such evenings." He noted my surprise. "Oh, I used to watch her from the hutch, William—even before I'd been engaged as a lookout. I was so afraid what might happen to her. The mesh over the pen could never hold off a determined predator."

I experienced a ridiculous twinge of guilt at the thought that he might have seen me creep out- side and observe Old Lavender myself on one such occasion. But the twinge passed at once. I was an adult now, and Spode was clearly treating me as an equal.

"The hollow where you spent so much time with her used to be quite a bit deeper, you know," he continued. "The wire was bent up in that corner, and even for a . . . " Spode faltered. "For a *goodly-proportioned* rabbit like your grandmother, escape was possible, though only if you squeezed very hard."

I recalled Spode's own successful escape to the cabbages. "Is that how you got out?" I asked.

"Yes. At around the same time she did—before they put the bricks under that part of the fence." He thought for a moment. "It was nearly twenty years ago now."

"She must have been really determined to squeeze that hard."

"Oh, she was! Suddenly, she was out. It was terrifying to witness. I watched the trees every second, of course. They were crisp against the moonlit sky. I would have been able to see the silhouette of wings, swooping down upon her and . . . "—he faltered again—"taking her away. She took just a few moments to get her bearings. Then she leapt briskly across the meadow, heading past the French memorial and onwards to the east wall. She didn't once look back. It's as if she knew exactly where she was going. *As if she were answering a summons.*" These final words carried a little extra Spode gravity, of the sort he used when trying to make a point that needed a bigger dose than usual.

"How long was she gone?" I asked, for Grandmother had obviously come back that time.

"She returned just before dawn," Spode said. "And she was . . . *changed,* somehow."

"Had she seen anyone?"

"She implied that she'd seen one of our kind." He paused. "And one of *theirs.*"

"A person? *Who?*"

Spode didn't answer.

I hardly knew how to react to all this. It seemed strange that Spode should be relating Grandmother's escapade of twenty years ago, and not her flight of the night before, into the storm. The thought of her heading off into that driving rain distracted me from Spode's story. And deeper questions lurked in the wings.

Old Lavender had never mentioned escape to me, past or future. She didn't live completely in the physical world, as you know, but seemed to come and go daily from some other, less earthbound place. Why would she go to all the trouble of escaping—of digging a hole, slipping past

Emmanuel or devising any other cumbersome means of liberation—when all she had to do was slip away in her mind? Besides me (and I say this with humility, as I was still an apprentice), the only other member of the colony who might have understood this was Spode himself, and even then, despite his erudition, his thoughts could be decidedly lead-footed.

Then he said something that has stayed with me always, though I'm pretty sure he was quoting Old Lavender: "At moments like that, William, when you muster the courage to attempt the unimaginable, the consequences are so often on your side. It's as if good fortune is actually programmed to coincide with great risk."

"But what happened last night, Spode? Did you see her leave? Did you see anyone else?"

There would be no more answers. Emmanuel's hand closed around me—rather meatier than Wellington's providential digit, I imagine—and just like that, my old life ended.

⁖

On the way to the market, jostling next to my companions in the crate, I tried in vain to digest Spode's story. Little about it seemed credible, least of all the emotion with which that fusty elder had told his tale. But emotions aside, I had to remember that this was Spode, archivist *sans pareil*. His attention to detail was legendary. If he said that Old Lavender had escaped many years before my birth, and that she had encountered another rabbit (along with a human of some sort), my instinct would be to believe him.

The farmer's truck trundled up through the woods and across the former Allied ridge. Heavy rain had turned the unpaved track into what it probably had looked like two hundred years ago. The truck dropped like a stone into brimming, artillery-sized craters.

The jostling shifted a few gray cells. I recalled that the moon had been close to full the previous night. And it hadn't escaped my notice that this was the month of June (although I couldn't tell you what date, exactly). Maybe Old Lavender had been preparing herself for this particular alignment of circumstance: Moon approaching full. Torrential rain. June.

We bumped past the Visitors' Center and Lion's Mound and turned left onto the Brussels road, and as the gray cells shifted again, I thought of the night I'd illicitly observed my grandmother: her heightened energies, and what surely could have been interpreted as intense longing.

And those shapes.

At the time, I could only explain them away as tricks of the air—visible exhales of the Hougoumont night.

As if she were answering a summons.

Had Old Lavender finally gone to join those shapes?

She couldn't have left by the same route she had taken twenty years ago, clearly. The fencing had been reinforced, and bricks added.

How did she get out last night, then?

I began to tremble as another thought surfaced: *Had someone taken her away?*

The truck entered the city limits and approached the market, and these questions gave way quite naturally to other, less specific ones, as if, my fate drawing near, the Hollow Way were meandering into a higher arena. The view was definitely better from here, that's for sure. And existential questions relaxed a bit: destiny's whereabouts didn't seem nearly as pressing as Old Lavender's at that moment, for instance. I couldn't help wondering, though: Is providence a relative thing? Is my providence—or yours, for that matter—less significant than the providence that had touched the Duke of Wellington?

Reassurance often comes from the most unlikely sources. As Emmanuel was grabbing for me in the pen, I distinctly remembered him saying: *"Allez, mon petit.* Everything will be all right." He seemed unusually well informed, and it did make me wonder whether Moon hides wisdom in simpletons for a reason.

I suppose that what happened to me at the *marché des abattoirs* could be called providential, even though the fate of Europe didn't hang in the balance. For how else can you explain being crammed into a banana crate with a heaving mass of your own kind one moment, and trucked to a Brussels market with a decidedly ominous name, and the next moment finding yourself in a quiet garden with two trees and a perfectly acceptable patch of grass? From hell to nirvana, you might say. And in just under two hours, including the transportation. I don't know. I'm over eighty in your mathematics, they say, and I still don't have an answer. The abattoir market does, as its name suggests, sell meat. But there are also vegetables, clothing, trinkets and pets on offer, and it was never clear if the items in this last category, when not sold in their living state, were then sent to the abattoir across the *place* to be sold as something else. How is it that I didn't have to make *that* momentous journey?

Doubtless something without physical substance—without four legs, two legs, or legs of any kind—was at work that day. Miracle, magic, randomness, providence . . . All I remember is that the shadow of a hand appeared over the crate and hovered, undecided. Someone said: "This white one, with the dots?" More hand-hovering. A skitter of paws as my relatives dove for cover. Then another voice, a deep baritone of the type that hums so pleasantly through the digestive system: "Well, all right. The dots it is, then."

Through such banal moments is destiny decided. Really. Don't forget that it rained hard on the night before the Battle of Waterloo and French artillery got stuck in the mud, thereby changing the course of Europe. (Though it's true that Napoleon might still have rallied if the Prussians hadn't turned up.) "The nearest-run thing you ever saw in your life," said Wellington.

Weather, Prussians . . . history is simply a set of precarious uncertainties. Your history and mine. I, for one, might have been a French rabbit instead of a Belgian one had the rain stopped.

But I digress.

Haggling came next. The genteel dispute over my fate joined the general din of deal-making in the market. So many fates decided in a single day! The deep, pleasing voice persisted, dulling my anguish at losing so kindly a buyer. At last a price was agreed upon, dispiritingly modest though it seemed to the merchandise itself. The Moroccan boy manning the stand grabbed at me—soullessly, as one would grab at a plucked chicken. Perhaps he felt he would have gotten a better price for me at the abattoir.

I was incarcerated in a small, white cage with nothing but cold metal underfoot, lifted high and then swung like a lantern through the crowds. Stares snapped my way. An occasional sigh drifted by, along with wafts of kebab and roast chicken. Perhaps I should have realized then that there was something different about me. I recalled what Grandmother had said, about me being like a bowl of water with a calm surface. Maybe these people were trying to peer into the depths.

A little arc of empty space opened around the cage and a queer silence fell all around. Merchants stopped yelling odes to their beautiful fruit; babies ceased crying; a man throwing empty wooden crates onto a pile with a sound like pistol-cracks turned to look. I would get to know his expression well over the years. Looking back now, I think that the sudden silence in the marketplace was just simple surprise—surprise that something as inconsequential as a rabbit might require deeper review. Is that wishful thinking on my part? Or vanity?

And what, exactly, guided that hand over the crate? I mean, why did the hand choose me, and not one of my brothers, or sisters, or cousins? All of them would have made just as good pets. But most, sadly, were probably served up with cranberry sauce and potatoes a few days later. Was it my looks—a white coat with that cryptic scattering of black spots? I hope not. One should never rely on looks. They may get you out of a scrape or two when you're young. But time will rush on, your coat will no longer be so pristine, and inevitably a scrape will materialize on which your looks will have no effect whatsoever.

Or perhaps it was Moon who had intervened. He's compassionate, no doubt about it. Rather like your god, I suspect. But there are flaws in his character. He's like an incorrigible, heavy-footed uncle for whom one feels love and exasperation in equal measure. He can make colossal errors, Moon. But on a good day, he's capable of great things.

I just cannot bring myself to credit mere chance, somehow. Chance is Moon's houseboy—a lackey, responsible for small delights like finding a blade of sweet grass poking under the chicken wire, or a dry patch of hay. Things like escaping the butcher or discovering love require higher powers.

I've heard humans say that fate comes knocking. Well, Moon never knocks. He either hails us pleasantly from afar, or he barges in. He'll send his eagles swooping down with only the gliding shadow of wings to announce them, often for no other reason than to keep us on our toes. You can find yourself very suddenly without a corpus if you're not light on those toes, believe me. But once in while, when the mood takes him, Moon sends something that delights. A fresh cabbage leaf, perhaps. Or a caressing hand.

6

It's strange that in your language, the word "home" is used for a palace, a box under a bridge, and every sort of abode in between. Is home an idea? I wonder. Or a locale?

For years after being so precipitously taken from my family, I considered home to be one place only: Hougoumont. I was convinced of this—certain that happiness had briefly been mine and would never return again. An ache installed itself, so persistent that at times I was hardly aware of it. But whenever I tried to coax myself to sleep with memories—with the odors of the meadow, or the rasp of dry leaves against chicken wire—there it was again, that ache, raw and throbbing and all that was left of my vanished family. Even the prospect of going to the Duchess of Richmond's ball rarely comforted me. I would set the scene in my mind, and begin to drift off to sleep, only to find that the door to the salon on Rue de la Blanchisserie was locked, the building derelict. I realized only then that I'd never gone to the ball alone; I'd always gone with the others.

I've heard that humans are rarely content with their homes. So many lust after all things big, it seems—castles, even—though they would probably manage perfectly well in a cabin with just a door and a window. Has anyone ever made a study of dwellings and happiness? I suspect not. Anyway, since humans always presume that big and expensive means better, I suppose a cabin would bring only meager satisfaction (and a good deal of embarrassment on the slog up the social ladder). No. Few would pass up the chance to live in a palace. No matter that there might be sixteen paces between the sink and the dishwasher, or that half a kilometer yawns between the settee and your bed. It's your possession—*your* kingdom. That's what counts, apparently. Though the first thing a rabbit would notice would be the draft.

How irritating—how exhausting!—such a place would be for us. Rabbits hate drafts, for one thing. For another, we would have to map out the entire half kilometer between the settee and bed to identify all the good places to hide along the way. We're prey creatures, don't forget; we probably think about hiding places as often as people think about money, so that gives you a fairly good idea of our preoccupations.

I feel a bit ungrateful saying all this, considering that I had a palace built just for me. A rabbit palace, granted, but splendid accommodation all the same. The ground floor is full of fresh hay, and a separate toilet alcove is piled lavishly with wood chips. An old wine box cleverly serves as a bedroom, and upstairs, there are two roomy shelves ideal for the long hours of reflection for which I'd been trained so thoroughly in my youth. The front door even has a latch.

My palace, though, had no soul at first. Nothing could have felt farther from my patch of earth at Waterloo.

I realize now that a vital aspect of home is the traces of *you* that are left there: the smell of your last meal; a you-sized hollow in the earth; a kernel of corn with your tooth mark on it. Nothing is more comforting than the remnants of *you*—certainly not grandeur, or the number of bathrooms, or even a roomy wine cellar. Thus I had to rearrange the hay in my hutch after it had been so carefully plumped up, and tip over the food dish all the time, as my proprietors never seemed to catch on that it's easier for us to eat from the floor. Pity that with all its superiority, the human brain is still unable to think like a lagomorph.

Even with all the distractions of this newfound luxury, I just couldn't banish my homesickness. The family tried so valiantly to help, overfeeding me, scratching the sweet spot behind my jaw, taking me into the living room to run around a plush carpet without the slightest scent of grass. But memory had the last word: Hougoumont still filled every sense to breaking. My new home was only a few kilometers down the road from my birthplace, after all. Old Lavender would have been able to tell you whether or not you could have heard the cannons from here. If it's true what she once said— that we live in relation to our memories every minute of the day—then surely, I thought, I might channel the power of my ancestral home to build some kind of future.

Instead, memory imposed on me a kind of half-life. My ears turned constantly, hoping to pick up the bold, steady hiss of wind that blew so freely over the Hougoumont fields—the sort of wind that breaks up into toothless eddies in city gardens. My skin felt moribund in the recycled urban air. I longed for the freshness of rain on my coat, but was locked in my cage at the slightest hint of a storm lest I catch cold.

And those smells of home . . . oh, where had they gone? Sometimes, if I closed my eyes, I could summon the vapors of the hutch: the sweet-and-sour reassurance of kin. I listened for the trickle of Old Lavender's digestion, and underfoot, on the cold patio tiles of my new place, I could feel the desiccated droppings of the enclosure. Was I experiencing that gift Old Lavender had talked about: the gift of reading things? Surely she hadn't meant basic smells and dried droppings. If I'd really inherited her gift, then I was supposed to uncover deeper meanings, as she had; to consort with them until I understood them. Old Lavender would have been able to stand in a new garden and read meaning in it at once; she would have interpreted such a drastic change in life as forward motion, and gotten on with things.

I wondered if it was simple coincidence that the garden had high walls, or just a bit of whimsy on the part of Moon. Hougoumont was walled, too. It's funny how familiarity pops up in uncharted places. If you think about it, our passage along the Hollow Way is often sprinkled with landmarks of similar shape and hue, like stepping-stones over a stream. These familiar objects are not random, but present themselves with a sort of intentional symmetry, as if pointing the way. Our passage from one to the other really should not be taken for granted. Think about the turns your life has taken (I mean *really* think—stare out a window for at least an hour), and you'll discover a startling, sometimes pleasing, invariably inexplicable logic in the way things have happened to you.

∴

My days began early. Just after dawn, when my hutch door was opened, I took my first constitutional. This involved a thorough sniffing of the air from the edge of the patio—an initial "study of circumstance," as Old Lavender called it. This rather arcane habit has gone out of favor these days, especially among the young, but the sad truth is that if Jonas or Caillou had been at all adept at the skill, they might have avoided their fates.

We rabbits have mediocre eyesight. We can see greens and blues best, along with shapes and shadows, which just about summed up this garden whatever your eyesight happened to be: a weed-in-

fested lawn; ferns drooping in dim reaches; two
trees, their trunks darkened by ivy; and foliage
that waved mysteriously, even without any wind. A
peony of sickly mien sulked near the patio. There
were holes in the wall here and there where bricks
were missing, and in one corner, a discarded toilet awaited removal. The pile of cracked plant pots
next to it looked, to my eyes, like the jagged end of
the Hougoumont chapel.

The garden was uninhabited except by me, but
not unvisited. So much of my day was spent taking careful note of the rustling in the trees (inept
rustling meant pigeons; arrogant rustling, mag-
pies, and so forth) and keeping an eye trained on
the tops of the walls. The dark red capping tiles
formed a handy walkway for neighborhood cats,
who lounged like petty sultans in the ivy massing
over one corner of the wall. I'd seen an occasional
cat at the farm. But these city animals seemed to
be the most distant of cousins. They were phony
predators, overfed and bored, on the lookout for
any sort of cruel amusement. I knew they could get
into the garden if they wanted to—I'd seen one pad
across the lawn one evening and exit by the back
tree. Inevitably, my fear of these domestic hybrids
soon supplanted my fear of hawks, a clear indica-

tion that the real natural order did not extend this far into town.

Without a colony to impose order or a grand-mother to rein in idiocy, caution ruled my days. My route through the garden was thus carefully planned and rarely varied. If it did vary, then the variation became the new, planned route. And so it went. Each route—or its variation—took in a thorough examination of the peony, the ferns, both tree trunks and anything at all that was unfamiliar or misplaced. Should one of the cracked plant pots have been moved, for instance, an olfactory once-over of the pot's new location was required. If a dry leaf had blown in over the wall from a neighbor's tree, this single leaf would need further investiga-tion. (Autumn was a particularly tiring time, as you can imagine.) Every route, no matter how it traversed the garden, was accorded that essential component of the rabbit universe: an escape plan. This might be a damp hollow behind the tree, or a concealed alley behind the begonias.

Such exacting habits also occur in humans, I believe. Wellington himself fussed for hours over his terrain. Not that I'm comparing myself in any way, but I do think that my hero and I would have sized up the same parcel of land with similar pre-

cision. The Duke rarely left the field during battle. He studied the topography closely—combed it
with his spyglass, and spent long hours reconnoitering on horseback to assess the circumstances.
He knew all the ridges and hidden dips, and the
tall crops of rye and corn in which men could be
shot without ever seeing their enemy, but which
also provided excellent cover and the advantage
of surprise.

Sometimes one can be too meticulous, however. The battle very nearly took a fateful turn
when Wellington rode down from the ridge to
the Hougoumont orchard early on the morning
of June 18 for a final check. He wanted to make
double sure that all his orders had been carried out
and everything was in place.

He halted on the track . . . a mere ten yards or
so from a French sniper.

The man, hidden in the undergrowth, didn't
fire. Had he even recognized his target? one won-
ders. Wellington had been wearing a plain blue
coat and cloak, after all. Perhaps, addled by circumstance, and suffering from a momentarily frozen
trigger finger, the sniper had had a change of heart.

No amount of vigilance can wrest control from
providence—or however you wish to call the powerful force that can, without notice, render even

history just a featherweight on the wind. From the mighty Wellington to a humble rabbit, outcomes maddeningly, inescapably depend on myopic snipers or absent hawks; on the thickness of the mud or a hollow under the fence; on whether or not the corn—or begonias—hold up as escape routes.

I was a lucky exile, I suppose. Many never know such havens as mine; many continue to wander in their hearts, even when the physical body has more or less come to a halt.

I have in mind a particular exile.

He's been lurking at the corners of these pages, and it's about time to bring him up, I think. He may not have troubled your reading so far, but he certainly haunts this story. He's never found his own, fragrant piece of earth anywhere. Oh, he tried to find it, all right. In every country he invaded. But you can't spend your youth at Hougoumont, as I did, and not grasp that bloodshed is no way to find a happy *chez soi*.

Napoleon.

The name will never have a neutral feel, will it? Somewhere in France at this very moment, someone is calling him a monster, while across the street they're toasting his deeds and singing "La

Marseillaise." Both extremes have a firm hold on the historical record, though paradoxically, both only give insipid impressions of the famous commander, and are about as cliché as the brooding countenance and hand tucked into the coat. Did you know, for instance, that Napoleon had a very keen sense of humor? Difficult to imagine in someone who felt that the world belonged to him, and then went doggedly out to prove it.

There's no shortage of speculation regarding Napoleon's legacy. I hasten to say that I'm no expert. But nothing is more satisfying than discussing a famous person who is maddeningly hard to pin down. Bonaparte's character, his marriages and affairs, his strategies, moods, illnesses and death all provoke the liveliest of debates, even now, though the subject was beyond the capacities of most of the lagomorph population at Hougoumont. Spode tackled it gamely. But his administrative bent narrowed his interests to dates, locations and names, which we all promptly forgot. *History is in the details* . . . Just not in Spode's, it seems. I'll try to recall Old Lavender's, therefore, as her lessons had that curious sticking power.

We'd all grown up in Napoleon's shadow as much as we'd grown up in Wellington's. The earth of our farm had received vast numbers of both armies into her bosom, after all. It seems simplistic to call one group of men good and the other bad, when they both ended up in the same spot, and in the same sorry state. The corpses of the French and British may have been burned in separate pits, but their ashes must have found each other on the wind eventually, and come to rest together. Now that I think of it, the tranquillity of our woods and meadows had an ambiguous feel: part victory, part defeat, the joy of one and bitterness of the other joined in common regret.

Grandmother liked to point out that the French and the British never fought each other again after Waterloo, and that the price for this might have been a reasonable one to pay. I'm quite certain she didn't believe it herself, though, but was just encouraging discussion, which was commendable. Because of all the occupants of our colony, she was the one who understood how high the price of Waterloo—and Hougoumont—had been.

Old Lavender loved military strategy, as I've mentioned. I even suspected that she deeply admired Napoleon's genius in that sphere, though she'd never admit it. But grand military design always paled before her little historical pearls.

"Napoleon was a wreck when he arrived in Belgium," she said. "Oh, there were flashes of his old Austerlitz brilliance, certainly: he managed to humbug Wellington with that surprise attack on the Prussians near Charleroi. But the poor man was a digestive nightmare. He was ill, in pain. Imagine having to ride a horse with those terrible hemorrhoids—even a sweet-tempered mare like Desirée! He would explode at underlings, then sink into lethargy. That kind of thing."

"Spode says he was a psychopath," I ventured, pleased not only that I'd retained this bit of information, but that I'd found the opportune moment to disgorge it.

"It was not that straightforward!" Grandmother retorted. "Napoleon was a complex man. One shouldn't judge complex people." She paused. "One should stand clear of judging complex rabbits altogether."

Is she touchy because I'd mentioned Spode? I wondered. *Or because she was being soft on Napoleon?* These were delicate questions. History favors the distinction between tyrants and heroes and one is expected to stick to them. Old Lavender, ever the contrarian, liked to toy with the boundaries.

"Labels never did anyone any good," she went on. "They make life so anemic; they destroy so many intriguing paradoxes. Napoleon was voluble, moody, choleric. Everyone knows that. But all of a sudden, he could be tender. He talked with nonstop agitation. Then he'd sink into depression and not talk at all. He was a poor sleeper and tended to wander about at night, reading, catnapping, snacking." Old Lavender continued with pride in her tone, as if she were the first historian to have come up with this particular observation: "He would have made a great creative artist, Bonaparte—a painter; or, being French, a chef— if he hadn't been so bent on creating war."

"You said he could also be kind."

"Of course! The worst tyrants can show kindness . . . even genuine kindness. Avoid labels, William!"

And with that she recounted a little tale:

At about two o'clock in the morning of June 18, Napoleon was sitting in an upper room of Le Caillou, his headquarters down the road from Waterloo. He was unwell. He'd been writing dispatches, and had ordered horses to be brought at seven o'clock. But his attitude was one of great physical and mental suffering.

At length he struggled down a steep ladder and ordered his page, Gudin, to help him into the saddle. The boy lifted the emperor's elbow too abruptly, and Napoleon pitched over to the off-side, almost falling to the ground. *"Allez à tous les diables!*" he hissed. "Go to the devil!" And with that he cantered off in a rage.

Gudin fought tears as he watched his master ride away with members of his staff. But to the page's surprise, the emperor had only gone a few hundred yards when he came riding back, alone.

He placed a hand tenderly on the lad's shoulder and whispered: "My child, when you assist a man of my girth to mount, it is necessary to proceed more carefully."

The page became a general, and eventually fell during the Franco-Prussian war.

I wasn't sure what to make of the Napoleon of that story. In such a short space of time, the man demonstrated a full spectrum of emotion. I began to imagine that he might, indeed, have harbored different personalities in his short, squat frame. I think you call it schizophrenia. I don't know. If that were the case, then Boomerang would also have to be labeled schizophrenic, as one never knew when he was going to suddenly hurl himself against the barrier; or Jonas, for that matter, who could be wit and charm personified, and then stab some-one from behind with an insult. I suppose that if behavior leads to serious death and destruction, then it needs to be given a serious name. And seri-ous punishment. Though I do wonder if the British had gone a bit overboard after Waterloo, sending Napoleon to St. Helena.

The Royal Mail ship takes five days to get to St. Helena from Cape Town. Even today, not many people venture there. The island is a primeval remnant of basalt, shrouded in vapors and rising up from the sea like a jagged thought from sleep. "This cursed rock," as Napoleon called it, was from all accounts as bleak a place of banishment as his captors could have wished. Longwood House, where the emperor lived out his days until he died there on May 5, 1821, at age fifty-one, sits on a damp plateau buffeted by trade winds and prone to smothering mists. Napoleon would pace the porch for endless hours, waiting for breaks in the fog and scanning the horizon for passing ships. To keep boredom at bay, he luxuriated in long, hot baths while reading, or dictating to a page. Formal dinners were staged in the cramped dining room. The meal was rather like an off-color operetta for an audience of sycophants, served on Sèvres porcelain by liveried butlers, candlelight glancing off the silverware, while the counterfeit court, shorn of all validity, still bowed allegiance to their castaway.

Just the thought of Longwood House made me feel more at home in my own exile. No rabbit could have endured the damp vapors of Napoleon's last residence, after all. And I do think that of the two deportees, I was luckier with the accommodation, though there were times when a myopic outsider might have confused us: like Napoleon, I paced the edge of the patio, trying to pick up scents from home. I scanned the tops of the walls, hoping for a bearer of news. When the northern mists descended over the ash trees, my bones ached, as I'm sure Napoleon's had.

Even as he fretted and pined, however, the emperor wasn't beyond dropping compliments. The following one was related to me by my grandmother, and as I repeat it now, separated as I am from my beloved Hougoumont, the words have a special ring. One exile comforting another, you might say: "But for the heroic determination of William, the Prince of Orange, who, with a handful of men dared to stand firm at Quatre Bras, I would have taken the English army in *flagrante delicto* and would have conquered."

7

Was I afraid of my new, alien patch of turf? Oh, terrified! The walls soared high . . . so high that they seemed to lean ominously inward. Light was a scant commodity. The lawn itself was just a scrappy rectangle, bald as a newborn rabbit in places. Though not the windy plain of Waterloo, the garden did contain a harmonic of sorts that I couldn't interpret. At first I rued this lapse in my gift. But soon I realized that the air could not move freely here, and any reading of the circumstances, as Old Lavender liked to call it, was necessarily hampered.

This hidden harmonic turned out to be just as frightening as the predators of Hougoumont . . . or even the threat of Napoleonic plunderers. This was my new Untried, you might say. But even if my cage door was left open during the day and I was free to wander wherever I liked, the risk of stepping off the patio into that inchoate space always seemed too great. For you see, whenever I stood there alone, contemplating my very own Untried, all I could think of was what had happened to poor Caillou.

His shriek resides in me still.

But at last I did it: in a triumph of will I banished Caillou from my mind and stepped off the patio!

At once my haunches turned to water.

Caillou reappeared immediately. I looked up, as indeed he seemed to be urging, and imagined a hawk with the wingspan of a vulture. In vain I searched for a sign from Old Lavender. How could she have summoned the courage to enter the Hougoumont meadow, alone, and at night—*twice*? I even cast about for a signal from Moon himself, assuring me that I had nothing to fear; that I would certainly return to my hutch from this excursion in one piece. ("One piece" meaning, of course, without bloodied, shredded flesh. Why is reality always reduced to insipid niceties?)

The Untried lay before me, ripe as a cabbage. For the first time in my life I was poised to take a bite.

The light had begun to fail. *When the sun touches the tops of the trees it's time to go home, William.* The voice jangled a distant nerve, then vanished.

Heedless, I crept to the center of the grassy patch, where something familiar suddenly gripped my body. That old impulsiveness surged. Exhilerated, I felt pulled towards the tree at the back corner as if by a knowing hand. (The hand also, thank heavens, bestowed a last-minute dollop of self-confidence.) Behind the tree yawned the sort of long, dark, narrow space of earth to which every rabbit feels an atavistic pull, but which I'd never seen myself until that moment.

No, William.

The warning seemed closer now.

I rose up on my hind legs and peered behind me. Old Lavender must have been present in some incarnation or another, for she then raised her voice with typical surliness and snapped: *Go back! It's late. Remember Caillou . . .*

It's interesting to recall the first time one breaks step with a mentor. We all have to grow up, after all.

It was in that garden, at dusk, when I felt it for the first time: the voice of the old sage being drowned out by another, more resonant one. Instinct? Destiny? No matter. Far more compelling was the sensation of finally acting on that wild streak in my blood. The impulse was so strong that I found myself wondering if my white Hougoumont ancestors had ever spent any time outside the hutch.

Whatever it was that spurred me ahead, I'd completely forgotten the mindless choreography of the herd. For once I was acting entirely, gloriously, alone.

It was late October. The light was already slinking away over the walls, leaving just a few stray shafts in the greenery. A cozy, yellowish glow arced out from the house, but I'd ventured far beyond it, and anyway, the house lights only served to darken the rest of the garden.

I was craning my neck to sniff behind the ivy when I heard it: that soft, terrifying *thurrup* of wings.

Instinct took the upper hand. I flattened myself against the earth, rigid as wood. My heart beat at a speed unknown to humans. The tips of my ears turned cold. Was this what Caillou had felt, I wondered, at the moment the hawk floated in? But why bother to ask? I'd soon find out for myself.

The wings descended somewhere near the

peony. I glanced sideways in the general direction of the disturbance. One thing struck me: the relative ease with which my mind was functioning at that moment—relative, that is, to the utter rigor in my limbs. In a flash of déjà vu, I recognized the fear I'd known when venturing out by the full moon to observe my grandmother. But thoughts of the Hougoumont night also fueled a curious resolve. Now that I was removed from my birthplace, I had a moment (enhanced, I realized later, by the presence of doom) to reflect on one of those vintage Old Lavender tenets: something to the effect that someone else's predicament is almost always worse than one's own. For example, our kind generally has only the usual night predators to worry about. Waterloo combatants, on the other hand, had had snipers and skirmishers to contend with, not to mention mud, clogged weapons and fatigue, and regardless of whether it was death or survival that had greeted them at battle's end, those lads had gone forth gallantly and accepted whichever hand was extended. Surely, then, I could face whatever awaited me under the peony.

I also remember wondering about my new proprietor, and whether she'd been wise in her choice of rabbit. I was glaringly white, after all. Caillou had only been pale gray, and he'd been visible from across the Waterloo battlefield.

There was a vigorous scattering of earth, as if by an impatient beak. Then with horror I saw a small shadow detach itself from the peony's larger one and skip with purpose towards me (though stylishly, I couldn't help noticing). Death has many guises, I reminded myself . . . especially winged ones . . . and so I made myself even flatter, awaiting my fate. Should I speak to it? I wondered. Negotiate in some way? It was difficult to imagine Caillou surviving even this long in the proceedings, so I ceased to wonder what *he* might have said or done.

Before I could determine anything more, however, there was another *thurrup*, a rustle of ivy and the thing was gone.

I went faint with relief.

But I had to admit that there'd been a strange measure of grace about those wings, as if they'd belonged to something not intent on dinner. Was this my gift speaking? Had I read the air correctly? I knew that I couldn't afford to get poetic, though, stranded as I was at the back of the Untried . . . and at twilight, no less.

Someone came out of the house calling my name. Rabbits don't usually respond to that sort of thing, sensing as we do a trap just about everywhere, so I was reluctant to emerge from the shadows. I was found easily, though (I would have made a lousy foot soldier in the end), and gently locked in for the night.

How I longed for warm bodies that night! For musky smells, and the nocturnal whispers of Hougoumont. The sound of the beech branch would have been most welcome, even with its suggestion of phantom drummers.

I wasn't entirely alone, however. Old Lavender still felt close by, lingering somewhere in the ectoplasm. *What had happened to her?* The question stalked my sleep each night, and greeted me every day upon waking. Would I ever know the answer?

I tried to imagine the confusion in the colony after I'd left—after the farmer had headed out the North Gate with the load of us, and the dust had settled on the lane. Everyone in the pen would have been milling, taking stock. Maybe Spode, with his newly minted seniority, would have chosen a solemn moment to deliver the news.

Old Lavender, gone! Would there have been chaos? Insurrection? I considered the way that Grandmother had hectored everybody at one time or another and decided that some in the colony might have even breathed a sigh of relief at her departure. I could imagine the rumors swirling:

Had the rabbit in the moon bewitched her? Or a wild lover?

Alone, in an unfamiliar hutch, I simply couldn't ward off the vision of that moonlit night: Old Lavender standing on her hind legs like a young doe, and the specter of something moving against the south wall. Curiously, there'd been no scent on the air. No sound. Just the odd feeling that Grandmother had seemed to recognize those shadows—perhaps had even encountered them before.

I hunkered down in my new home, confused and lonely. Existential questions crowded around me like annoying relatives. Old Lavender drifted near:

There are sometimes no explanations, William. So don't try to find them, or pretend that they're there. They aren't. But there's always, always a way forward.

As it turned out, finding my way forward in exile would take more than an occasional visit from the disembodied Old Lavender. Solitude is the absence of others, one would say. Therefore, using that classic definition, my solitude in Brussels was almost as pure as it comes. I had my proprietors, of course—not to mention the presence of those elusive, *thurrup*ing wings, which might have belonged to something resembling company—so the definition was blurred slightly. Nevertheless, like Napoleon on his cursed rock, I had never felt lonelier.

I'm not usually prone to quoting Berthe, but as I'll probably never see her again, her remarks have taken on some poignancy, especially now that I was no longer a candidate for relieving her own solitude.

"Solitude is a state of being, William," she said once at Hougoumont. "There's a big difference between being alone, and feeling lonely." I even remember when she said this: We were jostling near the supper dish one evening, sandwiched up against Jonas's tail. Berthe was being unusually forthcoming, I remember thinking, and had I been able to escape her I would have, especially as her topic implied a need for attention. "How lonely one can feel in a crowd!" she sighed, shoving Jonas ineffectually before continuing. "Everyone pushes past me. No one looks me in the eye. They couldn't be bothered about my ideas."

All this I understood. With some remorse I remembered that I'd treated Berthe like that myself. I had looked her in the eye only once and never again, because she'd confused my politeness with ardor and it had taken me weeks to shake her off.

Just as we reached the supper dish, she said something disturbing: "I'd rather be a ghost, somewhere out there"—she indicated the meadow— "than feel invisible in here."

I remember that I'd glanced at Berthe's drooping jowls—not her finest quality—and then out through the chicken wire into the gloaming. "Have you actually seen them, then?" I asked.

"Only Old Lavender has," Berthe said. "You have to have her gift to see anything out there."

A chill passed through me and I said nothing. I'd never breathed a word to anyone about the gift I'd supposedly inherited from Grandmother. Nor had I ever connected it with anything actually visible—apparitions, for example. I pressed against the fence and shot a look at the place near the south wall where I'd seen those moonlit shapes.

Twilight was a particularly atmospheric time in the meadow, and it wasn't difficult to imagine all those battlefield ghosts going about their evening business. The traffic of souls was brisk at that hour, according to Old Lavender. She once mused that to fill the idle eons, the ghosts had formed various clubs to keep themselves occupied: cricket for the British, boules for the French . . . that sort of thing. So if Berthe's wish came true and she actually joined them, she might very well encounter the same large crowds outside the hutch as inside— and the same loneliness. Death solves a lot of problems, but not all of them.

But I've strayed from my subject.

"No one encourages reflection anymore," bemoaned Grandmother during my Hougoumont years. "These days, contemplation is reserved for misfits . . . or for those who chew their cud for a living. Our species can produce first-class thinkers, especially in captivity. It's just that you cannot be too comfortable. Comfort makes you sluggish and unimaginative."

I knew what was coming.

As if to prove her point, she would turn her rump to the fence and gaze at the interior of the pen. This meant that I, too, had to shift my position against her, which was most uncomfortable.

Jonas would look up from his digging with his usual insouciance, taking care not to look directly at Old Lavender. He may have been a rake and a cad, but in her presence he was reduced to the same obeisance as everyone else.

It would take several attempts for the question to audibly pass my incisors: "Why are you turned this way, Grandmother?"

She usually went into a deep trance during

these pen-gazing episodes, and it would take a good half hour for her to resurface.

Finally, on one occasion, she explained:

"I'm finding beauty in ugliness," she said.

The others stopped their nudging and mingling. The oracle had not only stirred, but reoriented her rump, a rare combination worthy of note. The rest of us might reorient our rumps for a stiff wind, an overly ardent suitor, or to avoid Emmanuel's lethal boots at feeding time. But when Old Lavender shifted her rump, she actually had something to say.

I examined the interior of the pen: there was plenty of ugliness to go around. Along the side of the fence facing the derelict dovecote, the earth had a darker hue from constant urination. Rotting seeds floated on the water dish; the hutch hadn't been cleaned in over a week and Spode, a stickler for cleanliness, had pushed some of the soiled hay out of the door. Berthe, usually more discreet, had left a scattering of droppings in the mid-foreground and everybody passing by felt they had to follow suit (an ancient lagomorph ritual), resulting in quite a rise in elevation. Even beyond the pen, there were no breezy fields to see in this direction, just the crumbling bricks of the courtyard wall and Emmanuel's rusting bicycle, dumped on its side with the back wheel immersed in a puddle.

Finding ugliness wasn't the problem. Beauty, however . . .

In a rare moment of affection, Old Lavender turned to me and said: "You're puzzled."

I nodded.

"William, the art of solitude is to appreciate your surroundings."

I nodded again. This much made sense.

"Any surroundings."

My eyes fell on the droppings. This made less sense.

Old Lavender sank back into her trance. It was another hour before she surfaced again.

"Make ugliness fascinating," she said, following my gaze. "Yes, even a pile of droppings. Then you're hooked. You know . . ."

How well I knew her "you knows." They usually preceded a lecture of fair length, punctuated by the usual periods of silence, which meant that lunch would be delayed by at least an hour. Here's a short version:

" 'Boredom' is a word invented by humans and used exclusively by them. If you can turn your back on beauty and still find the world interesting, then you have it made. Every important lesson can be learned from the simple tools at hand. Remember this, William. Because you may find yourself in far more challenging surroundings someday. Don't let dreariness spoil your spirit."

"How do you do that, Grandmother?"

"Well, let's begin." She rearranged her haunches, letting off a potent broadside of smell. "You can use any object as a springboard. Even common waste."

I regarded the growing hill of droppings. (Berthe had just made another contribution.) The word "springboard" didn't come naturally to mind.

"Now look at the droppings square on. Come, William!" Old Lavender nipped me lightly on the shoulder. "Focus yourself. Good. Now, slowly, carefully, move your gaze around the object in question."

I studied the dark, glistening mass. Like most rabbits, my near vision was dim; and anyway, I wasn't exactly sure what there was to look at.

"Take in the general size and shape, the bulk, that sort of thing," Old Lavender continued impatiently. "As if you had to draw it."

I did this, wondering idly what artist would draw such a subject. At once I felt my thoughts slow to a more comfortable tempo. The exercise felt a bit like our childhood studies of the chapel—a meditation that was supposed to open up a space in our minds into which light could shine—but this procedure felt much more refreshing and meaningful in comparison (the pile of droppings notwithstanding).

"Run your eyes over it several more times," Grandmother said. "Are you doing this? All right. Now, let your eyes follow an invisible circle around the pile. Then increase the distance between object and circle. Slowly!" she chided. "And don't get distracted! Do you feel lighter now?"

In fact, I was beginning to feel rather dizzy.

I tried the slow-circling again. Strangely, as if stirring from a long sleep, something moved within—a rising feeling somewhere in the region of my gut. I'd eaten well that morning, so I knew it wasn't indigestion.

Grandmother could tell at once that I'd felt it. Not only that, I'm certain that she knew I *would* feel it. She wasn't called an oracle for nothing.

"*Ugliness. Sublimation. Appreciation. Contentment.* Follow these four signposts as best you can."

Eagerly, and with considerable fascination now, I pinpointed each piece of ugliness in the pen and tried the circle technique. Before long the soiled hay, the putrid water dish and even Spode were easily encircled, brightened, and transformed into a sort of lightness of being generally reserved for higher mammals.

"There you are," Old Lavender said, sensing my elation. "You've now experienced true beauty: the letting go of the physical. You usually feel a bit lighter looking out at the fields, don't you?"

"Yes," I said. I hadn't thought about it before, but she was right. One did get a lift from the landscape—even from Waterloo's *morne plaine.*

"Well, you may not always have fields to look at. So you must find the lift in whatever happens to lie before you."

"In droppings?"

"In anything."

∴

Thanks to Old Lavender's rigorous schooling, after just a few weeks in my new home, I began to experience results with the circling technique. Not miracles, mind you: the garden was still too unfamiliar. Still, I managed to transform the peony into a thing of elegance at least once. And after a few months, the missing bricks in the garden wall began to look like loopholes. Not a sublimation, exactly. But a very comforting transformation all the same.

8

On nights of driving rain I always dreamed of Hougoumont.

I'd already been living in Brussels for some months and had hoped the dreams would have stopped. For gradually, day by day, I was pulling away from the clutches of homesickness.

And yet something still worked on me. Memory, of course. But also an unpredictable, Hougoumont-inspired quickening of the air that often happened in the early evening. There was no doubt that my birthplace had begun to settle into my bones. The images, sounds, smells . . . all had filtered deep—as deep as the roots of the chestnuts at the South Gate. Perhaps the Hougoumont I had taken away with me was already turning itself into that power source Old Lavender had spoken about: the energy of a beloved place or idea being put to good use.

The creations of sleep can never be controlled, however.

Heavy rain, then, always brought on the same dream:

It was the night of June 17, 1815. I was sheltering in the great barn. Despite the darkness and mud, supply wagons were splashing up the lane and passing through the North Gate. Troops bustled to and fro in nervous haste, their lips pale with cold and fear. It seemed that I could even smell their wet uniforms, rank as an uncleaned hutch. I perceived it all from the high seat of my dream, though logic prevailed even in sleep, and I found myself somewhere in the vicinity of the rabbit hutches.

I drifted outside into the courtyard, free as mist now, protected by the strange largesse of dreams through which a white rabbit drew no attention to himself whatsoever in the midst of preparations for the Battle of Waterloo.

The atmosphere was charged with the certainty of tragedy about to unfold, and the foreboding chilled me utterly. My breathing felt shallow. Men shouted above the din of the rain, and I detected a quaver in the top notes, as if their hearts had already acknowledged that they would soon kill . . . or be killed. It was as if I were stranded with them on the very knife-edge of circumstance, with only the flaccid grasp of Moon to keep me from falling. (I hoped that the men's god had had a tighter grip.)

I knew from my grandmother that Hougoumont sat in a strategic position coveted by both the French and Allied armies. Wellington had occupied the property first and was determined to hold on to it. The soldiers initially posted to the chateau-farm—two to three hundred men making up the light companies of the Coldstream and 3rd Foot Guards—had recently acted as part of the rearguard on the retreat from Quatre Bras and were completely spent. Stifling heat and humidity had been as merciless as the French.

I watched from the safety of sleep as the farm's defenses were shored up against imminent attack. The Guards faced a Herculean task: smashing loopholes in brick walls; barricading gates and doors; building fire steps inside the garden walls on which soldiers could stand to take aim. Any piece of wood would do: even chateau furniture was hacked apart for the cause. There was little food on offer. Few could sleep. Rain continued to fall in torrents and the temperature plummeted. The deluge soaked soldiers from both sides equally, though at least the Hougoumont defenders could take occasional shelter in the chateau and outbuildings.

Wellington personally supervised every detail of the preparations. But even he could do nothing about clogged muskets, or hands bloodied from gouging loopholes with bayonets, or the purgatory of sodden wool, rubbing the skin raw.

It seemed I could feel the rain against my own skin at this point, even in sleep . . .

An ensign of the Coldstream, Charles Short, was there: "We were under arms the whole night expecting the attack and it rained to that degree that the field where we were was half-way up our legs in mud; nobody, of course, could lie down. The ague got hold of some of the men. I with another officer had a blanket and with a little more gin we kept up very well. We had only one fire, and you cannot conceive the state we were in. We found an old cask full of wet rye loaves which we breakfasted upon."

No one, not even Old Lavender, could have put

themselves into Charles Short's boots—or into any of the other tens of thousands of boots that had filled with mud that night. But it's possible to stand where they once stood . . . to imagine what they had seen. You don't even need rain and mud to feel what I'm talking about. You just have to let yourself go very still, at your core, and the moment will do the rest.

Now go there: venture into the silent heart of Hougoumont.

That seething night is closer than you think.

Don't move . . . cobblestones gleam underfoot in the pelting rain. Close your eyes . . . mallets crack against stone; shouts pierce the orchard and echo through the barns. In the bleeding light of coach lamps, figures scurry to get ammunition out of the rain and into the chateau. They skirt the chapel, as if it were just another farm building, and you wonder why they don't slip in for a moment.

Because for so many of them, these would be their final hours.

∴

One morning, worn out from one of those dramatic preparation dreams, I slept most of the day and awoke to a calm, dripping evening. A little ramble wouldn't go amiss, I thought.

The rain had finally stopped and a pleasant somnolence enveloped the garden. I'd lived long enough with my new proprietor to know that this sort of evening was more conducive to romance than danger in the human lexicon. Much to my dismay, I'd begun to understand this lexicon quite well, even embracing some of its excesses myself, though the excess in question—promenading at night—was a mortal sin in our world, and probably the most egregious of all.

The rain had left a few cool breaths of mist lacing the shadows, and a sopping lawn underfoot. The frondy leaves of the ash trees, made tremulous by the slightest breeze, hung eerily motionless. Only the occasional, rasping drip from one leaf to another measured the evening's adagio.

I made my way to the garden's wide-open center and hesitated. The grass had already soaked the fur of my undercarriage, making it unpleasantly heavy. The sun had set early . . . twilight was faltering. I was breaking every rule of the rabbit canon.

I looked up: beyond the wall, a star blinked faintly through the grayish wash of city light. Perhaps it was the same star that had hung over us as we filed into the hutch at night. How I'd always longed to stay outside under the great vault of sky! Now here I was, doing just that, but the vault yawned coldly, and though I was apparently a reasonable student of circumstance, I felt illiterate in the face of such grandeur. For the first time, I thought of Moon in more subtle colors than the usual black and white. We'd always been trained to think of him as the chief arbiter of life and death—clear-cut conditions not requiring a lot of subtle shading. I mean, you're either alive or dead. That sort of reasoning.

On this blurred evening, however, I imagined a superior being of softer, more companionable hues. Dun-colored, perhaps. With little brown spots on his jowls, like Spode. And with some sort of weakness, such as digging up spring bulbs just as they're sprouting and then suffering from bloat. I considered that with such a stressful job and so few holidays, Moon might enjoy a rest on such an evening, when there appeared to be a lull in the life/death business.

Old Lavender hove unexpectedly into view. Normally I would have smelled her coming, but in this incarnation, she was curiously fragrance-free.

William! Stop being an idiot. Get back to the hutch at once! She'd never been one to mince words. Anyway, how could I forget the lesson she had drummed into us—the lesson learned from Napoleon's care-less ebullience on the morning of Waterloo? The emperor's leisurely breakfast in the face of battle was just the sort of rash behavior Grandmother was always warning us about. "We shall dine in Brussels tonight!" Bonaparte had proclaimed, even ordering a well-done shoulder of lamb for his supper. But of course, he never dined in Brussels. He didn't dine anywhere that evening.

According to one of his personal aides, Jardin Aîné, Napoleon left the battlefield not long before midnight and was on the move all night. Around four o'clock the next morning, after passing through Charleroi, he stopped to warm himself by the fire of a bivouac. He said to General Corbineau: "*Eh bien, Monsieur*, we have done a fine thing," to which Corbineau replied, "Sire, it is the utter ruin of France." Napoleon shrugged his shoulders and turned away. Haggard and drained of all color, he accepted a small glass of wine, and a morsel of bread that one of his equerries happened to have in his pocket. He then remounted and galloped off.

All right, so Napoleon suffered from hubris along with all his digestive miseries. He paid amply for it, though, didn't he, with that lousy dinner?

∴

I'd fully intended to get back to the hutch after Old Lavender's admonition. Something detained me, however.

I don't know what, exactly.

I studied the recesses of the garden through dim eyes. The shreds of mist seemed to be coalescing now, as if they may not have been purely atmospheric in origin. Was I using my gift and reading the air? I shivered. The suspect mist was only one step removed from the concept of ghosts, which had never sat very well with me. I knew that Old Lavender had seen them from time to time, at the far end of the meadow. She was never quite sure whether they were wearing French or English uniforms, but the point was, she said, that whoever they were, at least they weren't shooting at anyone.

The *thurrup* came out of nowhere.

"Well, well." The voice was cool, aloof. "Venturing out in the dark, are we?"

My response was a quaking thigh.

"I've been watching you lately," the voice continued. "You're finally letting your guard down, I see."

"Who . . . who are you?" I stammered, more rudely than I might have had the apparition introduced itself properly. This couldn't be a hawk, I consoled myself. Hawks have no time for chitchat.

The creature stepped closer, flipped a wing, then cocked its head in an elegant tilt. "I never bother with names," he said, for I could tell by now that it was indeed a "he," a blackbird, and more urbane and forthright than any blackbird I'd ever seen.

I'd noticed blackbirds come and go from the garden. They were usually in such an earnest hurry, which made them seem more like emissaries than residents. But just after dawn, and just before twilight, the air stood still, and at those moments they lingered. The entire courtyard of walled gardens became their open-air basilica then. They chose chimneys, topmost branches or the spines of roofs for platforms, and from there they staged the most mellifluous plainsong. Sometimes they warbled quieter fare, as if thinking aloud, or answered each other from opposite sides of the sanctuary. I never knew what, exactly, they were singing about. But the greater emotions were unmistakable: passion, lament, reverie, exultation. These bards of the half-light could soften anything—even extreme loneliness like mine.

"It's taken you a while to drum up the courage to explore at sundown," the blackbird said. He shifted his weight delicately, sidling to the right, then to the left, as if thoroughly reviewing me.

"My kind never explores at dusk," I said. I was about to tell him that my name was William, but as he had said himself, he wasn't terribly interested in names, and anyway, I was rather put off by the fact that he seemed to have been observing me for some time without my knowledge. "Aren't you afraid of the cats?" I added. It was a childish challenge.

"No," he said. "They're quite stupid, and useless parasites. But one must be careful all the same."

I glanced away. This creature seemed cultured—at least to someone of my humble breeding. And he spoke with a wry twist unexpected in a master of serious melody.

"I've heard singing like yours where I come from," I offered, making conversation. "It's exquisite."

He ignored the compliment. "Where are you from?"

"Waterloo. Hougoumont, specifically."

"Waterloo . . . "

"Yes!" I hadn't heard the word pronounced since I'd left home. "Do you know it?"

He said: "The road to Waterloo is just over there, behind those houses. The Chaussée de Waterloo, as it's still called. Wellington himself passed that way. The Pelouse des Anglais is very close by, you know. 'The Englishmen's lawn.' It was named after the cricket match Wellington's soldiers played there on the eve of the battle."

I glanced beyond the wall at the silhouettes of chimneys and gables cut against the night sky. "I didn't know that," I said, stunned to discover that all along, I'd been living so close to the road that led back to Waterloo . . . to home. I could hear the rush of passing vehicles from the garden, to be sure, and an occasional horn or ear-damaging siren, but I'd never imagined that such banal noise could suggest exalted destinations.

Forgetting my visitor entirely, I lifted my nose to the sky and tried to imagine the sound of horses' hooves and carriage wheels.

"You know about the Battle of Waterloo, then?" I asked, though the blackbird oozed sophistication and it was obvious he would know something about local history.

"Nature never truly recovers from human cataclysms," he said distantly.

I was flabbergasted. To hear Old Lavender's words recycled in this way, by someone I hardly knew, was astonishing, especially when he added: "Every creature who was anywhere near Waterloo sensed what was going to happen. The experience was passed down the generations through collective memory, right up to the present day."

I observed my interlocutor more closely. There was something about him I couldn't quite place. He seemed not only well versed in history, but to be moving gracefully to its rhythm. He had about him the aura of another epoch. In a playful moment, I even considered that his bearing would not have been at all out of place at the Duchess of Richmond's ball. The way the creature was turning his head and flicking a lustrous wing conjured all the courtliness of that event. In another incarnation, he might have been a prince. Or a duke . . .

On a whim, I decided to call him Arthur ("the Duke of Wellington" seeming a tad too formal). Just to myself, of course, as he didn't seem keen on introductions, and I wasn't sure about his sense of humor. He was somewhat aloof, with that touch of superiority so discouraging to less adept conversationalists like me. I hunkered down against the wet grass and swiveled my right ear in a fair imitation of Old Lavender, hoping to appear more sophisticated.

"Do you have collective memories in your own family?" I ventured.

The bird tilted his head. (A bicorne hat would

have looked quite dashing on it.) "My great-uncle lives with his family behind the parking lot of the Wellington Café, right on the edge of the battle-field. Humans have short memories, don't they?"

The question jerked me from my air-reading pretensions. I'd passed the Wellington Café in the farmer's truck on the way to the *marché*. I suppose I'd been too engrossed in my reflections at the time to consider the callousness of building a café on a scene of carnage.

"People lounge on the terrace, drinking their coffees," Arthur went on, "clueless that they're fac-ing a field where the rye was completely flattened by corpses of their own kind, shot and hacked to death. Oh, they think they know what happened there. But their evolutionary progress seems to be in reverse. They gradually forget the magnitude of what they've done—or at least, they've man-aged to disguise their violence as glory—so even-tually, in the course of time, they can no longer feel what still hangs in the air. Not the way we do. So they don't have any qualms about build-ing cafés on burial grounds. They've never really stamped out their zeal for warmongering—quite the opposite, actually. They can't seem to get enough of it."

I sat up straighter, impressed that some of the

lessons from my rather insular upbringing might be shared by more worldly creatures.

"Anyway," Arthur continued, "this uncle of mine had a grandparent, who had a cousin, whose very distant grandfather witnessed Quatre Bras. That's how we keep our memory going."

"I was brought up by someone like that," I said dreamily. "I mean, she was an expert on Waterloo. She also has a special . . . well . . ." I paused. "*Gift.* She—my grandmother—can read those things you were talking about. In the air, in the soil . . . everywhere."

The mention of Old Lavender seemed to interest the bird. He approached me, his jet-colored feathers gleaming opulently through the hazy air. At that moment, Arthur didn't seem to be a bird at all, but a being of stature, refinement. The namesake I'd given him out of sheer whimsy actually seemed to suit him.

I allowed myself a moment of reverie at the thought of the Wellington Café. The place was just up the valley from Hougoumont. The Duke had ridden his chestnut horse, Copenhagen, across the very field Arthur had described. (A coffee might have been a welcome addition to that breakfast of hot tea and toast, come to think of it.) I knew from my grandmother that Wellington's strategic ridge had been located just beyond where the tourist attractions now stand. In fact, the great conical mound with the lion on top was constructed with earth taken from that ridge.

I chewed absently on a dry leaf and considered Arthur's oversized personality. It seemed to me that maybe the human sect I mentioned earlier might have a point after all with its wheel of life: that maybe we shouldn't be so quick to dismiss birds—or any other creature, for that matter—just in case, in an auspicious spin of the wheel, they may have led the life of a famous duke.

"Is she still living, your grandmother?" Arthur asked.

"Yes!" My heart surged. Then the old Hougoumont ache washed over me: "Well, I'm really not sure."

In truth, I hadn't had any news of the physical Old Lavender since I'd left the farm, though her other manifestations were not infrequent. I'd already experienced unprecedented boldness that evening, venturing into the twilight. My audacity had been handsomely rewarded by this extraordinary encounter. So it seemed only natural to ride the wave and ask: "Would it be possible, as you are airborne, to find news of her? She's called

Old Lavender. And there are other family members, too . . ."

Arthur stepped closer, as if approaching a partner for a dance. He then turned suddenly and made a rush across the lawn. "Old Lavender," he muttered. "Hougoumont. I'll do my best."

And with that he rose effortlessly to the top of the wall, fluttered his tail and was gone.

There are only two things in life, William: earth and sky. We live in one, then we go to the other. There is no in-between. This ancient rabbit philosophy is still taught in some traditional colonies. I grew up with it, and never questioned it. But as I watched Arthur skim off into the twilight, part wing, part air, I found myself wondering about my received wisdom. For here was a creature who actually seemed to inhabit the in-between—and with such ease that I imagined him slipping casually from earth to sky at least a couple of times during the day, and again for his evening amusement, without showing the slightest sign of fatigue.

I trudged back to the hutch, my sodden fur anchoring me securely to earth. As the sage said, there's no in-between for rabbits.

9

It took some years of training after leaving Hougoumont to successfully practice what Old Lavender had preached about finding beauty. Fundamental to her teaching was the art of solitude, so it was indeed ironic that my persistent state of solitude usually occasioned only chronic heaviness, and not the lightness of being at the crux of her lesson.

Ugliness. Sublimation. Appreciation. Contentment. I just couldn't get past the first signpost, somehow.

One afternoon in late summer, I was circling my gaze around a particularly unattractive patch of mold on the wall when Arthur sailed in.

I whirled about, flustered. "I was involved in a delicate mental exercise before you scared me out of my wits!"

He made a gallant step backwards and apologized.

I stared hotly back at the wall. The mold hadn't budged. In fact, it was uglier and more offensive than ever, and as far as I could tell, would always be so. The last object I had successfully used as a springboard to the spiritual had been the discarded toilet, and that was three weeks ago, when in a rare moment of transfiguration a ray of sunlight had fallen directly on it. Old Lavender would probably have considered that cheating.

I set to grazing not far from where Arthur was spearing a patch of bare earth. We continued like that for some time, chewing and spearing in silence. Arthur seemed subdued, serious. I'd noticed that, together with the rest of his kin, he had almost entirely stopped singing, a sure sign that autumn was approaching and the frivolities of spring were about as far away in both calendar directions as they could be.

Finally I braved the question. Funny, isn't it, how the things we are most eager to know are so often the things we don't want to know at all?

"Do you have any news of Hougoumont?" I asked.

Arthur quick-stepped across the lawn, then made several elegant, dance-like moves towards the peony and back. With his formal attire and urbane poise, he was suddenly so much like his namesake that my opinion of the human animal momentarily brightened.

"I went there myself," he said.

I stared at him. "But it's several kilometers away!"

"Clearly you don't have wings," he quipped, stretching one out langourously.

My spirit soared. I couldn't believe my good fortune, standing nose-to-beak with someone who had actually been to my birthplace! Breathlessly, I ran through a roll call of every member of the colony from my time there, using the most vivid descriptions possible in case Arthur had dismissed them all as just a bunch of faceless rodents. "You know, the one who bounces off the fence . . . " and "Surely you noticed the elderly gentleman, and the homely one with drooping jowls . . . "

"Yes, yes," Arthur said, discreetly impatient. "I met all of them."

I hesitated.

"Well, all but one."

We paused as Old Lavender's name silently registered. Somehow I knew she hadn't come back.

"She was never seen again," Arthur said softly.

"She disappeared on the night before I left," I said.

How long had it been? With difficulty I tried to assemble the years I'd been gone from Hougoumont. But I had no idea how long I'd been living in Brussels. City seasons don't seem to have the same dimensions as country ones, somehow. Or perhaps it's just that all the dramatics that mark country days—wind, rain, snow, ice, darkness—are shrugged off as nuisances in the city and life continues regardless, though it's a pale half-life in comparison, in my opinion. And though I lifted my nose to the sky countless times a day in the city, studying the circumstances, each time the cycle of the year finished and the seasons began again, I grew more and more hazy as to how many cycles had gone before.

"I heard news in the woods near the old sunken way," said Arthur. "Something big happened at Hougoumont, apparently."

The tips of my ears went cold. "What do you

mean?" I assumed he was not referring to the big thing that had happened at Hougoumont two hundred years ago. Most animals have a slightly more modest interpretation of that adjective than you people do. "Big" describes being hauled off to the abattoir, for instance. Not a major European battle.

"Something . . . *inexplicable*," Arthur answered.

"Inexplicable?" My voice was barely audible.

"I had the same reaction," he said. "And I'm not one for fanciful stories."

It was true that Arthur was a consummate pragmatist—something about his relentless efficiency, I suppose, and singularity of purpose. But then again, there was that poignant singing. He couldn't have been entirely without fantasy.

"The weather was awful on the night your grandmother disappeared," he said.

"Yes, yes, I know! I was there." I was impatient for new facts. "It was probably as bad as it was in 1815! The moon was almost full, too, though there wasn't much light through the clouds . . . What else did you find out?"

"There was a sound from the rabbit enclosure."

"What sort of sound?"

"A groan. Or a sigh. Something like that."

I gasped. "Someone opened the gate!"

"It makes a distinctive sound, apparently," said Arthur.

"Yes . . ." *How could I have missed it?* I must have had my head buried deep, indeed, in the pile of snoozing relatives. My ears turned busily at the memory of the gate's doleful sigh. The lament of wood against wood had always meant only one of two things: that Emmanuel was finally coming to attend to us; or the farmer was about to take some of us away. I could think of no other reason.

Until now.

"So Old Lavender left by the *gate*?" I said. It seemed far-fetched, to say the least. The thought of the snoring Emmanuel, blundering from his bed in the middle of the night, struggling onto his bicycle and riding to the farm with the sole purpose of opening the gate to the rabbit enclosure was, of course, preposterous. Anyway, he never came to Hougoumont after dark.

But who else could it have been?

"Did you speak to anyone at the colony about this?" I asked.

"The elderly gentleman with spots."

"Spode!"

"That's him."

"He saw what happened to Old Lavender?"

"Yes," Arthur said. The single word thrilled

me, and yet my stomach sank with disappointment. *Why hadn't Spode told me himself, during that conversation before I left?* He had only elaborated on Old Lavender's escape from many years ago. I'd just assumed that he hadn't witnessed her adventure the night before.

"Monsieur Spode heard the sound of the gate," Arthur went on. I marveled at his graciousness in mentioning that old curmudgeon. "He peered out the hutch door to see what was happening."

I could imagine Spode, squeezing his way through the slumbering ranks to reach the door—really just a piece of metal grille hammered to a frame and fastened with a hook. (The grille had the added advantage of permitting some of the odors of the hutch to dissipate.) But I knew for a fact that you couldn't see very much through this opening—and certainly not the gate, which was on the other side of the pen.

"He couldn't have seen someone open the gate from the hutch door," I said.

"He didn't."

"So perhaps it was nothing." (Why do we say things we don't believe ourselves?)

"Stop interrupting and listen!"

I straightened up like an errant foot soldier. Arthur definitely had a commander's talent for tough love. Every nerve in my body obeyed him, and I didn't blame him for his rudeness, either. I imagine that Wellington had used exactly that tone when he told his men, just before fighting began at Hougoumont: "Remain quiet where you are until further orders from me."

Arthur went on: "Monsieur Spode claims he saw a two-legged shape retreating across the meadow with two smaller, four-legged shapes."

It took me a moment to process all those numbers. "Just after he heard the sound of the gate?"

"Yes. Spode was sure one of the smaller shapes was Old Lavender herself. It moved ponderously, at any rate. The other one . . . " he hesitated. "The other one Monsieur thinks was a pale-colored animal of some sort. The exact color eluded him."

"There was heavy rain and mist," I offered. "Colors can be tricky."

I couldn't remember how visible the moon had been that night. Even in torrential rain, the countryside had a certain luminescence by the full moon that it lacked when the moon was new.

I had no idea if this detail was as important to Arthur's kind as it was to ours. I wasn't aware of there being a blackbird in the moon, along with the rabbit that's already there. At any rate, with all this singular activity in the Hougoumont meadow, it seemed possible that perhaps Moon himself might have played a role of some sort. Could he open gates? I wondered. If so, what had taken him so long? There'd been rabbits at Hougoumont for two hundred years, after all.

Again I considered the possibility of the slothful Emmanuel coming by: overcoming his fears of the Hougoumont night and embarking on a life-changing mission—you know, the sort that erases forever the low regard people hold you in—even if that mission only entailed the freeing of an elderly, misanthropic rabbit. I would have dearly liked to believe this version. I do think that Emmanuel, like everyone, has hidden qualities. And anyway, there was no other rational explanation for the gate-opening, or the two-legged figure, unless Waterloo had suddenly become a hotbed of rabbit theft.

A less rational explanation began to take shape. But loathe to venture into that territory, I said, resignedly: "Someone must have taken my grandmother away. Hougoumont is secluded. You saw that for yourself. Even before I left, the farm was in decline. Thieves were not unheard-of in the area . . ."

I felt too despondent to go on. Modern gangs occasionally roamed the sleeping hamlets around

Waterloo. They didn't have the cachet of Napoleonic plunderers, but they still sowed fear. They were always on the lookout for any object they could carry off and sell. Someone had even made off with the priceless crucifix in the Hougoumont chapel.

I began to tremble. Our enclosure could have fallen into the sights of some ne'er-do-well who had already done his principal looting for the evening; who might have spotted Old Lavender in the run, and amused himself with the thought of a nice pair of gloves—or maybe a meal. In her case, maybe two.

Arthur broke into my burgeoning gloom. "I don't think she was taken away," he said.

"*What?* Why?"

"Because apparently she and the other animal *followed* the person across the meadow."

This was unprecedented rabbit behavior— unthinkable for Old Lavender. My heart tripped: she must have left willingly!

"But who was the person?" I asked.

"Spode said that the two-legged shape was oddly dressed, and was carrying something . . . He couldn't see what."

Unspoken business hung over this conversation. The figure Arthur had described didn't sound like anyone I knew. Not the farmer. And not

Emmanuel . . . at least, not the Emmanuel generally held in low regard. And he—or she—didn't fit
the description of a plunderer or thief.

The less rational explanation had circled
around and come back again, it seemed.

"Does your kind have a god?" I asked Arthur,
not as obliquely as I'd intended.

"Just a beacon of sorts," he said.

"Can that beacon open gates?"

"No."

This was what I would have expected from
the cool-headed realist, until he added: "That is,
I didn't think so until I went out to Hougoumont."

I stared at him, not sure if Arthur was simply
speaking of the collective memory he believed lingered around Waterloo, or of something else: the
shadows against the south wall, for instance. Or
the Hougoumont atmosphere itself, thickening
into a particular, identifiable shape.

"You felt it, then," I said. "That presence in
the air."

"Yes. But I don't feel the need to identify it
the way you do. A presence can take many forms,
after all."

Where did that leave us? I wondered. The gate
had been opened. Old Lavender and an unknown
animal had followed an unknown human form

across the meadow. The human form was carrying something unidentifiable. And no one came back.

I reflected briefly on Spode; I remembered the torch he had always carried for Old Lavender, and my criticism of him softened. For only then did I realize the anguish he must have felt. He had observed the object of his ardor depart willingly, never to return. And he hadn't even been outside on lookout duty, where he might have dissuaded her. In neglecting to tell me about these things, he had betrayed his remorse, and his bitter, aching jealousy, more clearly than any words ever could have.

Arthur broke my train of thought. "Monsieur Spode did say something else."

I hesitated. "What?"

"He heard a tapping that night. I asked him if it was a branch. Or a piece of fence in the wind."

"Yes, yes," I assured him. "There's an old beech at the south wall that makes that sound. Especially when the weather's bad."

"Maybe. But he said that the tapping was different than usual. Too regular. And it didn't correspond with the wind."

10

This is a particularly painful episode, involving hotheadedness, stupidity and a complete misrepresentation of one's dreams.

After years of being left behind when my proprietor's family went on holiday, a summer finally arrived when they decided to take me along. And it wasn't just a jaunt outside the city—a trip up the Chaussée de Waterloo to see my old home, for example, which I would have loved. No: This trip was an odyssey in both body and spirit. And

though the family's destination may have been
Normandy, mine was very nearly much, much farther: as far as the stretch of green ambrosia at the
end of the Hollow Way.

I traveled in the same little white cage in which
I'd been brought home from the market. Poetic,
isn't it, taking the unsuspecting innocent on a fateful journey in the same vehicle in which he was
rescued from the abattoir? Vaguely circular, philo-
sophically speaking. A metaphor for the Way, perhaps. In retrospect, maybe I should have prepared
myself better, as I felt ominously like Napoleon on
his gentle white mare, Desirée, taking a benign
mode of transport to imminent disaster.

How splendid the destination seemed at first!
The house was, in fact, a chateau, in which the
owner—a gentleman farmer who spent much
of the day riding around on his tractor, mildly
inebriated—rented out a few rooms. Even Jonas,
one of those tiring, bigger-is-better individuals,
would have been impressed.

The experience began with a significant vibra-
tion: a feeling of déjà vu without the "vu" part. That
is to say, I'd spent my early years in the shadow of
a phantom chateau—Hougoumont—that in our
epoch existed only in the historical record. Thanks
to French artillery in 1815, I'd never actually seen

it. All our young lives, therefore, we'd only imagined its life story . . . its genteel flourishing and epic demise. We could only inhale the air near its vanished walls and from it build our own, weightless Hougoumonts.

So up until that day, when the family car rounded the last bend of the drive in Normandy, I'd known only a ghost chateau.

But here was the real thing: turrets, balustrades, windowpanes glinting like a thousand eyes . . . Inside, there were acres of parquet, frescoed ceilings so remote you would have needed Wellington's telescope to make them out, and other luxuries that don't necessarily make life more comfortable. They just make you tired.

Getting from water dish to sleeping quarters in that place required a map and a compass. There were thirteen paces between the fridge and the sink. Thirteen! That's a long way to go to wash lettuce. It was a servants' kitchen, no doubt, where maids trod holes in their shoes on behalf of the gentry, idling upstairs in drafty salons.

At night I slept on the kitchen floor in the little white cage. But in the daytime, I went outside. And not just any outside, either: this was a vast parkland with soaring woods, a lake, uncultivated fields and untamed winds. The sensations were far more insistent than any I'd known at Hougoumont. Here was the Untried of all Untrieds. Even Jonas might have balked at the idea of venturing out into it.

The owner erected a fenced run for me, and for a hutch he refurbished a large wooden box which, he said with an ironic turn to his lip, had once been used as a meat container. It was kind of him, really. I mean, not many rabbits enjoy indoor *and* outdoor accommodation at a French chateau—especially when they're not expected on the dinner table.

Within seconds in that improvised run I felt it: that stirring in the gut I'd tried to stifle in my youth . . . that mysterious, wild gene I'd experienced in action during Old Lavender's moonlit escapade.

We'd of course lived and breathed outdoor smells at Hougoumont. But even when a tantalizing scent reached us on the wind, or a cryptic signal beckoned from beyond the trees, the general effect was diluted by the stench and chaos of the pen.

But here . . . here . . .

My gift for reading the circumstances, and that hot drive in my blood, were on a collision course.

I felt powerless to choose between them.

It was as if I'd spent my whole life waiting for this moment. My haunches were weary from constantly rising up and trying to catch things on the air. How Old Lavender had managed it at her age, I can hardly guess! Odors that I knew well—dandelions, for example—flooded the senses. Even with my dim vision I could see why: just beyond the fencing lay an entire, hallucinatory lawn of them.

Ah, yes . . . How well I remember my dandelion lesson.

"Life cannot be lived secondhand, William." (Old Lavender again.) "No one can truly describe a dandelion. You must experience one yourself— even if it means taking a risk. And you can't say you've really lived until you've taken at least one risk. Can you?"

I remember thinking it odd that she had added that little question at the end. She knew that I'd taken a risk with that open gate at Hougoumont. Did she actually think I needed to take any more?

Do you really want to be like Jonas, William? was another question Old Lavender used to ask, and one that now emerged in full interrogatory splendor as I gazed through the fence at wild Normandy. I was full-grown by the time I'd realized that I really didn't want to be like Jonas. But here I was, middle-aged, still asking myself the same question.

And how Jonas would have lusted after this view! Beyond the chateau, the vista increased in excitement incrementally. Since the rabbit eye is designed to spot approaching hawks and not the ants underfoot, this rolling-out of the view was a particular bonus. Beyond the dandelions—nirvana enough for anyone—more lawns beckoned. Farther still, meadows of long grass glistened, of the sort that had been recounted by our long-eared bards since the dawn of our history. This glorious Untried was broken only by a ring of forest towering at the very edge of my vision, like the gateway to another solar system.

My blood rushed; my heart thrummed. I was briefly reminded of leading the colony, the doomed Caillou in tow, out of the open gate, and my head cooled slightly. Jonas probably wouldn't have even blinked at the memory, however, and suddenly I wanted to be like him most keenly.

I can't for the life of me remember how I found myself in the dandelions. One moment I was in captivity; the next, I'd gone wild. Literally. There were no holes under the barrier. Looking back, I think I must have leapt onto the roof of the hutch and scaled the fence from there. I then crept across the drive and entered the green kingdom. *This is it!* I thought. The Untried stretched in every direction. My body hummed and flexed with an energy that all wild rabbits must feel, but that had been bred out of me countless flabby, bowl-fed generations ago.

Hubris surged. I even briefly, giddily imagined

that I was at the center of the universe, and that everything was spinning around me.

Rather as Napoleon might have felt, come to think of it.

Indeed, Bonaparte had built his agenda around the presumption that he was, in fact, at the center of the universe—*his* universe, fashioned to the dimensions of a colossal will and ego. He wrote conquests into his weekly plan as one would a routine lunch or dinner. Spain, Austria, Belgium, the Netherlands, Russia, Egypt (and I probably left something out) . . . *Which shall I acquire tomorrow?* It all would have made an impressive universe indeed if Bonaparte had actually been able to hold on to it. He certainly tried. "Power is my mistress," he declared. "I have worked too hard at her conquest to allow anyone to take her away from me, or even to covet her."

Well, I never worked that hard at anything. But standing where I was, on the threshold of a territory that would have fueled Napoleon's ambitions even further had he been closer to my size, I can say that a certain lust for adventure seized my loins.

Until I remembered that Napoleon had also said:

"One never climbs so high as when he knows not where he is going."

By now I was lost.

Look up! Read the circumstances! The old edicts bat-
ted like random flies. I barely noticed them. Oh,
I could feel the danger in every pore, all right. I
knew that there were hawks, owls, foxes, and more,
all very near. Worse, I sensed that they all knew
exactly where I was, and were just biding their
time until supper. You would have to be a very
myopic bird of prey indeed not to notice a white
rabbit in the middle of all that green. The thought
slowed me down somewhat. *Had I gone mad as well
as wild?* A nearby burrow of foreign rabbits would
have offset this foolery in terms of an emergency
exit, but I didn't smell anything, and even a tame
rabbit can detect the telltale fustiness of a burrow.

I made myself flat and immobile and waited for
I knew not what.

How far had Old Lavender gone, I wondered
vaguely, on the night she'd disappeared for good?
Had she found herself alone like this, in the middle of the Hougoumont meadow? Had she made
it through the breach in the east wall? Perhaps
she'd reached safety in a warren somewhere in the
barley field beyond, having bravely crossed, at her
advanced age, one of the great sites of the Waterloo
battle.

I'm not sure at what time I was officially
declared missing. By now I could hear my propri-

etor's children: the frenzy in their voices as they shouted my name, and the boozy owner himself, calling to them rather charmingly not to worry, he would ride his tractor all around the meadow to search for me if they wanted, but very slowly, so as not to run me over.

I found myself cowering somewhere near the forest, stranded alone in a place that felt completely wrong in the cataclysmic sense. That is, in the sense of a sandbar in a quick-rising tide. Or a serene valley before the tanks roll in.

Rays of late afternoon sun pierced the trees and lay in golden seams across the grass. A crescent moon glided into view, almost eagerly, as the summer sun would linger long yet. The thought of an eager moon was endearing, as if the universe may not have been the unfeeling place I was making it out to be, and I braved a wan smile. But then something began to weigh heavily— something significant, as if Moon himself, and not his namesake in the sky, had slipped past and placed a paw on my shoulder.

If something bad happens, William, chew through the problem methodically, as if it's a long, hard carrot. I'd like to think that this flash of Old Lavender wisdom was a portent, like the light of wisdom going on, but panic had replaced excitement as the cause of my shivering haunches and I was certain that if I was going to chew a carrot of any kind, it would be my last.

Old Lavender was not yet finished with me, thank heavens: *Square your shoulders! Take a step, even with all that despair pressing down. "Rise up!" Wellington told his men as they were hiding among the corn stalks. This you must do, William; you must rise up and face whatever life puts before you.*

I was just squaring my shoulders, preparing to rise up à la Wellington, when I saw it: a dark, irregular patch, floating down from the forest as if unmotorized. Just a branch, I thought hopefully, riding the wind. But there was no wind. And as it turned out, the dark patch had feathers instead of leaves, and soon I could see that its motor was of the most efficient kind, propelling it in my direction.

The "vu" was definitely back in the "déjà vu," because I'd seen this aerial maneuver before, near the South Gate at Hougoumont. The only difference was that back then, I'd been a spectator at the tragedy and Caillou had played the leading role.

Now I was the one at center stage.

Spode, Old Lavender, Jonas and of course Caillou himself all paraded before me, bemoaning my recklessness. I wondered what sort of arrogance could have drugged me like that—altered me until I'd had the temerity to consider myself a risk-taker on par with Jonas, and even, briefly, the center of the universe.

Anyway, it was good of them to turn out for my demise.

The falcon began his dive.

I'd always thought there wasn't much time in these sorts of situations. I'd seen the speed of Caillou's exit, after all. But when it's your own exit, there is, paradoxically, all the time in the world. Certainly enough time for the light of wisdom to switch on.

Old Lavender said that if you believe in something strongly enough, it very often materializes. I'm not sure if by "something" she meant the finger of providence, or just a particularly tasty dandelion, though you can probably imagine which one I was hoping for just then. I had my doubts about that particular piece of Old Lavender philosophy, however. The notion that Moon would limit his appearances only to those who truly believe he'll turn up would seem to relieve him of quite a bit of responsibility, in my view. If this were the case, then gods would have more time on their hands for general do-gooding, which they obviously didn't take full advantage of. As I trembled in that foreign meadow, nose-to-nose with destiny,

I considered—I hoped—I actually *prayed*—that Moon was better than that; that it really *had* been his paw on my shoulder just now.

Perhaps Napoleon had reflected along these lines just before his Waterloo.

A timely supposition, considering I was facing my own.

Suddenly, ridiculously, I was not afraid at all. In fact, I felt very, very well—content, even. Content enough to feel a twinge of regret when I heard:

"*There he is!*" It was the proprietor's young daughter, screaming and sobbing all at once.

"Where?"

"Over there!"

The falcon wheeled back towards the forest in a leisurely arc, as if his mission had been one of simple reconnaissance all along and he hadn't been in the least put out.

Did the near-cataclysm in Normandy change me? Old Lavender was a great believer in cataclysms as long as they were near and not complete ones. I was reminded of something she had said to Jonas after he was lifted, half dead, off the fence, his innards swaying in the breeze: *Disasters are often good things, Jonas—unless you actually die during*

them, though that's often not the cataclysm it's made out to be. In retrospect, maybe this piece of advice had not been quite as encouraging as Jonas would have liked. He did go through that odd transformation, though, so perhaps he had learned to look at life and death in a new way.

Disasters can even be entertaining. Oh, not really funny, per se, especially when the disaster is a complete one. Unless you're British, of course, in which case just about any sort of cataclysm can be rendered droll on the spot.

The battlefield of Waterloo offered some choice examples. Take the Earl of Uxbridge, for instance, Wellington's second-in-command and commander of the cavalry. Family scandal had prompted Wellington to treat Uxbridge with icy politeness, the latter having eloped with the former's sister-in-law. This painful personal history might have explained Wellington's laconic reaction to Uxbridge's predicament. When rusted grapeshot from French artillery struck the Earl's right leg, completely shattering it, he remarked to Wellington: "By God, sir, I've lost my leg!" Wellington replied: "By God, sir, so you have!"

The Earl was then taken to the village of Waterloo, where he underwent a gruesome amputation without anesthetic, but with a huge measure of bravery and good cheer. He complained only that "the knives seem rather blunt."

Uxbridge's leg was buried in the garden of the house in which it had been cut off. A mock memorial was erected with the inscription: "Here lies the Leg of the illustrious and valiant Earl Uxbridge, Lieutenant-General of His Britannic Majesty, Commander in Chief of the English, Belgian and Dutch cavalry, wounded on the 18 June 1815 at the memorable battle of Waterloo, who, by his heroism, assisted in the triumph of the cause of mankind, gloriously decided by the resounding victory of the said day."

Some years later, Uxbridge revisited Waterloo with two of his sons, found the table on which the operation had taken place and ate dinner off of it.

At least the Earl's chances of survival had been good—however dull the knives might have been. The stakes were far higher for me: four-legged creatures don't often lose a limb and survive, let alone go back and have a leisurely dinner at the same spot. I'm not sure I could have summoned Uxbridge's extraordinary good cheer if the falcon had actually grabbed me and lifted me high. All would have been over then—all good cheer in vain. The only remaining piece of agenda would have been the formal handing over of my essence to Moon, if that part is to be believed. But let's face it: if one has to cry out to something from the grip of imminent death, it may as well be to something rapturous, rather than (in my case) to an inebriated farmer unlikely to find you on his tractor.

After Normandy, I realized that perhaps I'd been too hasty in my judgment of Moon. Lately, I've even come to the conclusion that he is, on balance, a good-hearted individual, in spite of his flaws. Oh, I'd blamed him for what had happened to Caillou, all right (maybe to deflect blame from myself); I'd denounced him for letting me be taken away from Hougoumont and my family, and for giving me no sign that Old Lavender was all right. This is only natural for us: we don't hesitate to give our god a thorough scolding when life turns bleak. I only knew that I couldn't go on living in anger and remorse. That was no way to spend a single day—let alone the rest of your life. Nor was it any way to build a partnership with someone like Moon, whom you really don't want to scold *too* thoroughly.

Your god, it seems, gets credit for the good things but is never blamed for catastrophe. People assume there must be some deeper meaning in terrible events unfathomable to the human brain, and are content to leave it at that. Sterner cultures,

I understand, have even sterner gods, who wreak vengeance at the slightest provocation. I certainly understand the deeper meaning part. But not vengeance. That seems to be a human invention, not a divine one, and not something we have ever experienced with our god.

Well, never did I think that a small white cage on a cold stone floor in a drafty French chateau would seem like heaven, but it most certainly did after that adventure. I tucked into my store-bought dinner with almost religious fervor. For the second time in my life, kindness had visited me in the form of a human hand. Maybe I'd been too young to truly appreciate it the first time; maybe I needed two interventions to finally realize that the best dreams must sometimes remain intangible. That maybe we are better off gazing appreciatively at a green field, than actually finding ourselves in the middle of one. Dampness, darkness, exposure, falcons . . . this is what can happen to the loveliest of dreams.

Perhaps it's better to live happily with the idea of a dandelion, than to die eating one.

11

Every summer when I was growing up, on the weekend that fell closest to the eighteenth of June, an eager crush of reenactors would descend on the fields and lanes around Hougoumont. The original Battle of Waterloo occurred on a Sunday: an ecclesiastical paradox, you might say, as instead of praising their Prince of Peace, the assembled armies used the Sabbath for slaughter.

Picnickers, tourists, city folk and bemused locals would all crowd around the perimeter of the

farm to soak up the reconstituted glory of Napoleonic times. Uniforms, horses, muskets, cannons
. . . no detail was overlooked, except that there was
not a drop of blood anywhere, or a gram of fear,
which left us with the odd impression of watching a
clawless, toothless lion fighting a similar adversary.

"Sanitized war, that's what it is," Grandmother
would sniff when the cannons started up, practically shattering our eardrums. "Oh, the colors
and pageantry are nice. But it's meaningless without the hell that went with it. What's the point?
Where's the smell of fear? Of death?"

We understood her perfectly, being creatures
with supreme olfactory powers. It wasn't difficult
to imagine, on watching the mock soldiers wander about the farm in their brand-new woolen
uniforms, that during the actual battle even the
human nose would have been capable of picking
up the sour note of fear in the general perfume of
unwashed, sweaty bodies—a note singularly lack-
ing during the picnic-cum-war afternoons. While
it's true that the reenactments gave a pretty good
idea of how life was in the encampments—what the
soldiers ate and wore, how they slept and passed
their time and so forth—the attempt at actual war-
fare had a carnival feel to it.

"How realistic is it when people play dead, then

get up at the end of the afternoon and drive themselves home?" Grandmother would mutter. "At least they could dump a few corpses here and there for effect."

I never much liked that last quip of hers. For one thing, it reduced her in stature, making her seem more of a tabloid journalist than the high-minded thinker she was. For another, no casual Waterloo buff would want to spoil historical reconstitution with too much reality. Anyway, Old Lavender had described once too often the nightmare of corpses rotting in the June heat. She sometimes went into considerable detail before we slept, especially if we'd been troublesome that day, and believe me, it didn't make for a very pretty bedtime story. Nor was it something you wanted to confront on a picnic.

Every creature who was anywhere near Waterloo sensed what was going to happen. That those animals would have been terrified by the smells and sounds of battle is obvious. But how, I'd always wondered, did they sense the cataclysm *before* it happened? I could only imagine that so much destructive human zeal, multiplied by the thousands in a relatively small arena, had sent tremors through the earth beforehand that had bruised it forever.

Even the reenactments were sheer hell for small

animals. For our part, we would scrabble into one corner of the hutch, ears jammed into the huddle of fur in a vain attempt to dull the axe-blade of sound. Cannons, muskets, screams . . . it was excruciating. Some of us would even suffer a nervous tilt of the head for days afterwards. Nothing could dull the jarring thud of the explosions that hammered right through the floorboards into our sensitive feet, up our finely tuned digestive systems, and out through the teeth. It never even occurred to Emmanuel, poor dimwit that he was, to move our quarters for the event.

One such Sunday, I peeked out through the grille at the meadow, where, about halfway down the south wall, a British reenactor was just being "felled" after shooting blanks over the top of the wall. He landed gracefully—even artistically—in the plush grass (which would have been a formal garden in the original battle and a good deal harder). He lay still—very convincingly, I must say. I know this because I resolved to observe him until he got tired of the game. To his credit, this lasted quite some time, but in the end I outwitted him.

The Sunday soldier lifted his head, glanced around to make sure no one was watching, then crawled very slowly to the wall. There he opened a silver button of his uniform and pulled out a cell phone.

"Beth?" he yelled—he had to, as the din still raged all around, which meant that I could hear him quite well. "Beth? Oh, hi. I was just shot. Can you pick me up in the parking lot over by the café? Half an hour? Okay."

∴

War should never be entertainment, William."

We were back in our dusty hollow, Grandmother and I, the last reenactors having changed out of their uniforms and trundled off down the lane in their cars.

"What a sacrilege, playing dead in the very place where so many actually *did* die—and in such agony!" said Old Lavender.

The light was mellow, burnished. It would be one of those lingering summer twilights I so loved. The blackbirds, having retired sensibly to the woods across the valley during the theatricals, had already resumed their perches in the old beeches and chestnuts around the farm for evensong. There wasn't a single quaver in their voices, and it made me wonder whether their ancestors had been back on their perches on the morning of June 19, 1815, and if so, what they had found to sing about.

"It's amusing sometimes, though," I said, thinking of Beth and the rendezvous at the café.

"Humans learn to do this to each other," Old Lavender rejoined, ignoring my comment. "Therefore, one day they must unlearn it, before it's too late and all of them succumb to the same madness. It doesn't matter whether you're lagomorph or anthropoid: the crucial thing is to set an example. When is the last time anyone witnessed rabbits attacking each other en masse? Well, there you are, then. Lead by example, William. Lead by example. There's nothing glorious about war."

Oh, but there must have been some glorious sites in 1815! An illicit thought, I knew, so I kept it to myself. That didn't stop me from fantasizing, though: the sullen sun had finally broken over the battlefield by afternoon, gleaming on isolated breastplates and helmets as if they'd been hand-picked. The trumpets, the drums, the horses at full gallop . . . the distant staccato of "La Marseillaise" and shouts of "*Vive l'empereur!*" Now, *that* made for stirring bedtime stories!

∴

I t's easy to think such thoughts in your youth, on a golden twilight, in the safety of close kin.

But I grew up, as we all must.

I left home, and lived alone. I lost Old Lavender, and with her my compass. I couldn't even burrow into sleeping relatives anymore when the weather got bad. And though I had that power source—my birthplace—humming away deep inside, its energy was not always steady. Heavy rains would come, and with them that dream, and then the power source would churn like some ghastly turbine.

Hougoumont.

Whenever I awoke after that, it wasn't the sunny, carnival reenactment that filled my head, but rather all the lessons learned at my grandmother's side, drawn from the resonance of a single, monumental day.

∴

J une 18, 1815: dawn. Mists and driving rain continued, unabated, from the night before, wrapping Waterloo in perpetual twilight. The troops in and around Hougoumont were sleep-starved, waterlogged, filthy. Their French counterparts could be heard just three hundred yards away in the valley beyond the wood, faring no better. Fires smoked in the laden air, barely warming feet and tepid beverages. Voices rang out randomly through the fog.

Eleven o'clock . . . eleven-thirty . . . No one knows when, exactly, the first shots were fired. You'll recall that as we listened to Grandmother's stories, we imagined the village church bells chiming eleven times, so I'll stick to that interpretation.

Waterloo is small as battlefields go . . . the Hougoumont part of it even smaller. How extraordinary, then, that my farm—my tiny corner of Belgium, which even today people have difficulty locating on a map—should have made history in just a few hours.

There was a prelude of sorts for the hellish symphony to come: muskets crackled on all sides as soldiers tried to clear them of mud and damp. Men groaned their way out of the mire; called out wearily for a shot of gin; whistled to their chargers. Each new timbre and echo moved logically, inexorably towards the masterwork to come: a demon's creation that no human composer would ever admit to.

Combat raged in the orchard and all along the south wall.

By early afternoon, the chateau was alight.

In the words of Major Macready, Light Division, Thirtieth British Regiment, Halkett's Brigade: "Hougoumont and its wood sent up a broad flame through the dark masses of smoke that overhung the field; beneath this cloud the French were indistinctly visible. Here a waving mass of long red feathers could be seen; there, gleams as from a sheet of steel showed that the cuirassiers were moving; 400 cannon were belching forth fire and death on every side; the roaring and shouting were indistinguishably commixed—together they gave me an idea of a laboring volcano."

Wellington could see the conflagration from the ridge and sent a message down to the farm: *You must keep your men in those parts which the fire does not reach. Take care that no men are hit by the falling of the roof or floors . . .*

The wounded, having been dragged into the chateau for shelter, had then to be evacuated. Many didn't survive this extra jostling. Others could be seen crawling from the conflagration, their clothes ablaze.

A severed hand . . . a jawbone shattered by a musket ball . . . compound skull fractures . . . These were not even the gravest injuries that William Whymper, surgeon to the Coldstreams, treated on-site. Casualties were taken to the great barn or other outbuildings that hadn't been torched, and laid next to the wounded from both armies.

Strange, isn't it, how men who can fight, suffer and die in close proximity to each other have such difficulty actually *living* side by side?

For those huddling inside the little chapel, the Hougoumont flames would forever be remembered as sparks of grace, stopping as they had at the feet of Christ and harming no one.

The fighting at the South Gate was savage enough. But it was the North Gate—the very symbol of Hougoumont—that would go down in history. The gate had been deliberately left open for the passage of ammunition and supplies. Sometime around midday, the French forced their way down the lane skirting the west side of the barn and arrived at the North Gate.

Close it! a Guardsman screamed, electrifying all those mustering within. Together they threw themselves against the gates, scrabbling for a foothold in the boggy entrance.

Myth took shape in the form of a French attacker, Sous-Lieutenant Legros—"l'Enfonceur," or "the Smasher"—solid as an anvil, who hacked his way in with an axe. An infant myth found fertile ground and grew. Heroes sprouted at every thrust of the bayonet. *How many Frenchmen followed Legros through the gates? Thirty? A hundred?* Truth and legend are tricky bedfellows. Whatever the number, the Coldstream Guard slaughtered all of their foes and became legends immediately.

What did it sound like, I'd always wondered, such killing? Many a sleepless night I'd spent imagining the animal cries from across the courtyard: the crack of weapons against wood, against steel, against bone. And the smell . . . earth battered to sludge; sweat cloying as urine; the bitter, choking gunpowder, so thick that it practically obscured those massive gates swinging in the balance.

Somehow, in the melée, they were heaved shut. Wellington would famously say: "The success of the battle of Waterloo depended on the closing of the gates of Hougoumont."

And what about the drummer boy?

He was no footnote—not in our lives. Each legend has a beating heart, after all, and the drummer boy soon became this vital organ at our farm, even if, as you will recall from Private Matthew Clay, he had actually come through the South Gate and not the North, and during another skirmish entirely. What is legend, though, but history written in the way that moves us most? I'd grown up near the North Gate; I'd breathed the very exhale of its legacy. Over the years, that boggy spot had hardened like resin into an icon, and deep within this amber, far from anyone's control, the farm's preferred history will pulse forever.

Wellington's voice often fills my head, and I've listened to him many times as he extolled the crucial closing of the gates . . . *the* gates, through which the drummer boy simply *had* to have passed for legend to live on.

"*Please*, Grandmother," we would implore her. "What happened to the boy?"

We knew for a fact that he'd been spared by men who, at the height of the bloodletting, had still retained some notion of when the killing should stop; that Private Clay had escorted him to safety in the great barn, his drum gone. We knew in our hearts that the boy must have been mute with fear. Our souls shuddered at the thought of what he had seen.

After that, the legend dangled loosely. Occasionally it would even let out a mournful sigh, like the open gate of our pen, though the sound carried only fitfully across the centuries. *Did the boy escape the smoking ruins of the farm? Did he ever recover his drum?* Grandmother would only speculate in the vaguest way. "Perhaps he died of fever . . ." But the all-knowing silence that followed suggested more . . . much more.

Whenever the wind rose at night, and the old beech tapped its rhythms against the south wall, I thought about that elusive boy.

∴

June 18: dusk. The sun was shining blood-red through drifting smoke by the time Field Marshal Blücher arrived with his Prussians. The reinforcements had come in the nick of time for Wellington. One officer heard him declare: "Night or the Prussians must come!" It had, indeed, been a near-run thing.

Sauve qui peut! was the cry among the French. *Everyone for themselves!* The ailing emperor fled the field, his ragged army—even his magnificent Imperial Guard—scattering in disarray.

When the red ball sank into darkness, the looters came.

The moon was only a few days shy of full on the night of June 18, 1815. Historians rarely mention this fact, though Old Lavender, as you can imagine, took great interest in it. The human animal would have had more illumination for plundering—though the benevolent souls administering relief would have been able to see better, too. For those of my kind, catatonic in their burrows, the full moon would have brought some comfort, reminding them that a being existed who just might see them through this cataclysm (although obviously, until that point, he had let them down royally). It makes one wonder where *your* god was on that night, by the way. He must have let quite a few of his followers down, too.

They say you couldn't take a step on the battlefield without brushing against a soldier's body, quick or dead. Indeed, countless souls were still breathing at day's end, though most would not make it out alive, trapped as they were under an army of corpses whose ranks they would soon be joining. Some had fallen in impossible postures, legs folded underneath them, their agony sharpening by the minute. *Minutes . . . quarter hours . . . half hours . . .* Grandmother told us that time idled cruelly on a battlefield, toying with victims as a cat with birds, and that this was one of humanity's punishments—greater, even, than death. And the wounded perished not only slowly, but anonymously, their names dissolving along with them in the mud. Four days would go by before the last survivors, deranged by thirst, pain and solitude, were finally dragged off the Waterloo field to makeshift, flyblown surgeries.

Crazed horses plunged about the wasteland, or sat helplessly on their rumps, their forelegs blown off. Some ten thousand horses died at Waterloo; many were barely cold by the time locals arrived to strip these faithful servants of their meat.

Looters roamed this Armageddon like hyenas. Some couldn't even wait for the fighting to stop, but crept over the field with bullets still flying bright-eyed as zealots. Soldiers themselves took part in the desecration: they stripped still-writhing, still-bleeding men of purses, clothes, watches, pistols, swords . . . anything that could be sold or bartered. When the soldiers departed, the peasants moved in. Any victims who resisted were quietly knifed in the darkness; in their zeal, pillagers even killed each other.

I haven't mentioned the smell much, have I? You would think I would have, being a creature so inclined. But in truth, I realize now that the prevailing corruption was not what one would have assumed. No, it was the stench of greed. This is a phenomenon our kind has never actually experienced and I'm extemporizing here, but I do know of an example that might sway any of you still convinced of the glories of war: teeth, young and unstained, were pulled from the mouths of the dead and dying in such quantities that they would turn out to be a bonanza for the British denture industry. "Waterloo teeth," they were called, and many a wealthy customer wore the smile of a battlefield corpse.

.·.

*O**h, must I go on?*
I've run out of words. How can there possibly *be* any more? A great poet might find some, I suppose, hidden in a corner of the battlefield I've overlooked. Old Lavender was certainly never at a loss, her long silences notwithstanding. If I thought it would do any good, I would stop this chin-wagging and pray to Moon instead, asking him to erase the memory of those terrible deeds forever, for the sake of all the inheritors of Waterloo . . . and of all wars, for that matter. Which is just about everyone, I should think. But I don't know Moon very well, really. Few do. And one can never say for sure when he's going to be at home.

On the evening of June 18, Wellington rode back alone to the village of Waterloo. Here and there, moonlight broke through the clouds and fell in artful beams over the carnage, as if the final act of this tragedy had not quite ended and the house lights still burned. Wrote Charlotte Eaton: "He saw himself surrounded by the bloody corpses of his veteran soldiers who had followed him through distant lands, of his friends, his associates in arms, his companions through many an eventful year of danger and of glory."

Indeed, though he had miraculously escaped injury himself, Wellington came away more deeply wounded than anyone could have imagined.

At around three o'clock the following morning, Dr. John Robert Hume, Wellington's surgeon, paid a visit to his headquarters room:

"I went upstairs and tapped gently at the door, when he told me to come in. As I entered, he sat up in bed, his face covered with the dust and sweat of the previous day, and extended his hand to me, which I took and held in mine, whilst I told him of [Sir Alexander] Gordon's death, and of such of the casualties as had come to my knowledge.

"He was much affected. I felt the tears dropping fast upon my hand, and looking towards him, saw them chasing one another in furrows over his dusty cheeks. He brushed them suddenly away with his left hand, and said to me in a voice tremulous with emotion: 'Well, thank God I don't know what it is to lose a battle; but certainly nothing can be more painful than to gain one with the loss of so many of one's friends.'"

12

The road between Brussels and Waterloo was a charnel house unto itself. Historians tend to overlook this, but those of us of nostalgic bent who live near the Chaussée de Waterloo can sometimes hear, hidden in the sound of angry car horns, and in the descending whine of buses slowing for a stop, a long-vanished acoustic. When darkness falls and a lull occurs in the traffic, there it is: horses' hooves and wagon wheels, echoing along the mythical route beyond the wall.

Charlotte Eaton paid a visit to Waterloo just

a month after the battle. Intrepid lady that she was, she ventured with her party along the same road so recently employed by great men, anonymous sufferers, bold women and the dead. She'd already passed through Brussels, noting that it had filled up alarmingly with the wounded since her flight to Antwerp. Marked in chalk on every door was the number of casualties being harbored there: *un, deux, trois, quatre,* even *huit militaires blessés.* At every open window, Charlotte spotted victims of war, "languid and pale, the ghosts of what they were."

Heartsick, she made her way up the *chaussée.* Mile upon mile, a numbing succession of calvaries unfolded before her:

"Bones of unburied horses, and pieces of broken carts and harness were scattered about. At every step we met with the remains of some tattered clothes, which had once been a soldier's. Shoes, belts and scabbards, infantry caps battered to pieces . . . these mournful relics had belonged to the wounded who had attempted to crawl from the fatal field, and who, unable to proceed farther, had laid down and died upon the ground now marked by their graves—if holes dug by the way-side and hardly covered with earth deserved that name. The bodies of the wounded who died in the wagons on the way to Brussels had also been thrown out, and hastily interred . . .

"Deep stagnant pools of putrid water, mingled with mortal remains, betrayed the spot where the bodies of men and horses had mingled together in death."

The Eaton party alighted from their carriage at the very spot where British troops had bivouacked on the night before the battle. Corn was still beaten down, the earth still trampled. It wasn't difficult to imagine how swampy the camp would have been in torrential rain, and what misery had unfolded there. Charlotte ventured ahead a few paces and stopped short: a field of mass graves greeted them, freshly turned.

Such a jaunt across the *morne plaine* of Waterloo could be construed as voyeuristic, perhaps. Even ghoulish. But Charlotte's account has a feminine sensitivity which had clearly appealed to my grandmother, who insisted we learn this tale by heart. Through the forgiving lens of two hundred years, such a journey, if deeply felt, escapes judgment, it seems to me. The "glory" of war is often manufactured afterwards by male writers, after all, and not by the women, who are invariably left behind to pick up the pieces of their broken men, but who can read entire human stories in the torn sleeve or bloody hat in which men can only comprehend victory and defeat.

Come, let's stroll alongside Charlotte for a little while.

Stop beside her as she surveys the ruined land: the broken, withered harvest that had once stood six feet high; footprints left pell-mell in the clay and baked hard by the sun, bearing witness to the desperate struggles of horses and men. The surface of the plain is literally whitened by innumerable books and papers of every description: love letters, novels, muster rolls, washing bills.

Please, don't look away. Not yet. Gaze with her.

Pick up, as she did, one of those paper treasures. A volume of *Candide*, a pack of cards, a sheet of military music. "One German Testament, not quite so dirty as many that were lying about, I carried with me nearly the whole day . . ."

Glance down: an outstretched hand, only partially decomposed, reaches up from a grave.

Faint from bearing witness, Charlotte hurries off, only to find herself at Hougoumont, a still-open sepulcher.

"Melancholy were the vestiges of death that continually met our eyes," she wrote. "The carnage here had indeed been dreadful . . . At the outskirts of the wood, and around the ruined walls of the *château*, huge piles of human ashes were heaped up, some of which were still smoking . . . I took some of the ashes and wrapped them up in one of the many sheets of paper that were strewn around me; perhaps those heaps that then blackened the surface of this scene of desolation are already scattered by the winds of winter; perhaps the sacred ashes which I then gathered at Château Hougoumont are all that is now to be found upon earth of the thousands who fell upon this fatal field!"

I've often speculated about what happened to those ashes Charlotte Eaton had gathered so reverently. Did she tuck them away in her writing desk when she returned home? Were they thrown into the fireplace by some unsuspecting maid? Or did the lady have a change of heart, slipping out to a corner of her English garden one day and, when no one was looking, tossing the ashes into the wind, praying that they would be carried back across the Channel to their rightful home?

"Roads are symbolic," Old Lavender used to say, after telling the story of the Eatons' journey. "They lead us to great things, and away from disaster. They give us hope that there may be something better around the next bend. They take us home. Cloistered animals like us will never experience such a physical road journey, of course.

But I can assure you that our kind of journeys—
the sort you take without moving—are even more
adventurous and illuminating. Not always, of
course. Sometimes our routes are as rutted as the
chaussée. We can despair on them . . . die on them,
too . . . without anyone noticing. But if you don't
take them, you get nowhere. So rise up, William,
and step over the ruts."

On quiet evenings in the city I can sometimes
hear the Eatons' carriage, taking them up the
chaussée to my home.

∴

Battle is a precarious business—hit or miss,
you might say; a chain of events that almost
always goes wrong at some point or other, even for
the winners. Historians do an admirable job clean-
ing up the wreckage, to be sure. It's up to them,
after all, to survey the tangle of past centuries and
put things in order for the ages to come. They are
also not beyond a bit of editorializing: inflating
heroism; overlooking atrocities; obscuring com-
plexity by turning the vanquished into simplified
rogues.

If you'd spent your early days as I did, crouched
against the flank of a Waterloo expert, you would
deduce that history is really just a series of lucky

breaks and stupid errors, and a favorite haunt of providence. Take the Battle of Ligny, for instance, Napoleon's final military victory. The Ligny is a small but marshy stream about ten kilometers from Quatre Bras where the French engaged the Prussians two days before the main battle on June 18. Napoleon's plan was to wedge his forces between the British and Prussian armies, thus fatally weakening their alliance.

Only farmers lived around Ligny then, as they had for generations. Windmills dotted the landscape. The harvest would be a good one that year: crops soared as high as a man, as they were soaring at Quatre Bras and Waterloo. Human aggression seems fatally attracted to bucolic Nature.

The dozing villages of Ligny, St. Amand, Wagnelée and all their connecting hamlets shook brutally awake with Napoleon's opening cannonade. Combat soon raged from house to house, from hand to hand. Elderly residents cowered at their hearths, shell-shocked and speechless. Blücher and Napoleon had taken up observation points in windmills on opposing sides of Ligny, from where they could witness the fire and blood as a passing bird might, though without this creature's truly panoramic perspective.

Napoleon did manage to eke out a victory at

Ligny, it's true. But fate took the guise of Jean-Baptiste Drouet, comte d'Erlon, one of Napoleon's generals, who ultimately spent that June 16 marching back and forth along the dusty road between Ligny and Quatre Bras to conflicting orders, never engaging in either battle. Old Lavender (among many other scholars) is fairly certain that had d'Erlon's troops managed to fight that day—no matter where—the outcome of Waterloo might have turned in Napoleon's favor.

Don't forget that in 1815, communiqués between commanders and their armies could only be written on paper and delivered by hand. Usually a horse was also involved. Clearly, the resulting trio was not always reliable; it most certainly wasn't quick. And when more than one trio of paper, messenger and horse were involved—when, on the same afternoon, Ney ordered d'Erlon to Quatre Bras, Napoleon ordered him to Ligny and then Ney summoned him back to Quatre Bras again, with the hapless messengers sharing, ever so briefly, the same dust cloud as they galloped past each other—it would have surprised no one if the count had found himself irritated, saddle sore, and with some extra ammunition on his hands.

History is in the details . . . lucky guesses, a good horse, the weather . . .

Oh, yes: and digestion.

Few creatures understand this last criterion better than the rabbit, whose digestive system functions with the most precarious equilibrium.

Rather like Napoleon's.

Thus, chance roamed freely around the woods and fields near Waterloo, scattering unpredictability at every crossroads. I should have anticipated, therefore, an unforeseen twist in my own Waterloo history.

13

I hardly recognized Arthur when he flew in. I knew that he'd been busy, as an early spring green had brushed the courtyard, and his dawns and dusks were fully occupied with singing. But beyond the familiar tail-flicking and wing-thrumming, there was an agitation in his aspect that made me instinctively glance up at the walls. There must have been a predator about, I thought, and he'd come to warn me.

"I have news," he said curtly. (Wellington's

messengers may have used as few words, though they surely would have added "sir.")

Arthur said: "I have to start from the beginning."

"The beginning?"

"Yes. The day of June eighteenth, 1815. Specifically, the siege of Hougoumont. The beginning of your story."

My story . . . What was he saying?

Arthur stepped closer and stared hard at me. "The mystery of your past."

I experienced a moment of panic. It's true that I'd asked him to find news of my relatives—and of Old Lavender in particular. But his question seemed booby-trapped, somehow. The mystery of my past was another matter. I mean, how many of us really want to solve an enigma that occurred many years before our birth? The very mystery is what makes life so colorful and intriguing, isn't it? Nuance, illusion, quest . . . all seem much more agreeable than the scary unknowns of discovery.

I thought about the magic of Hougoumont, especially at twilight: the vapors that crept over the walls and into the garden, and the restless pockets of air trapped in the milkiness. How could I forget the shadows fingering their way over the grass, and the occasional tremor in the darkness, as if it had been startled? Would my memories be ruined by Arthur's revelation?

I squared my shoulders. Wellington would have. "Yes," I said. "I want to know."

He began:

"The fighting at Hougoumont finally stopped at about seven-thirty in the evening. Your grand-mother told you the details, I think. I don't need to elaborate."

Arthur's delivery lacked its usual elegance. He seemed anxious, as if he had to impart his news as quickly as possible.

"Sometime that afternoon, a young soldier led a boy from the South Gate to safety in one of the barns."

"Ah, yes, the South Gate," I mumbled to myself. "Private Matthew Clay." Then, to Arthur: "Grandmother would be glad that you made that distinction, because most people think that the boy came through the North Gate."

"Theories differ," Arthur said, rather coolly, I thought. He went on: "The air in the yard was suffocating. Everything was black with soot from the burning chateau. Flying embers scorched everyone. Horses went mad. Some of them ran the wrong way, straight into the fire. Livestock burned to death in their byres. There were many injured men in the barn where the boy had been taken— this was obvious to any creature by the prevailing odor of blood. And, of course, by the screams . . . "

Arthur paused with the drama of a natural storyteller.

"A surgeon was amputating limbs."

Another pause. Then: "No one knows exactly what happened to the boy once he reached the barn. The young soldier may have given him a corner of rye cake, or some tainted water. Maybe the fact of being only a boy saved him from certain punishment for being French. At any rate, he was left to his own devices. According to what I heard, when darkness fell, he emerged into the courtyard."

The next pause seemed a bit exaggerated, so I urged him on. "Yes? *And?*"

"And he was carrying a rabbit."

"A *rabbit?*" This development seemed anticlimactic, even for me.

Arthur ignored the comment. "A white one. There were rabbit hutches in the barn, of course. It was an estate, after all. There were gardens. Livestock. The gentry would have raised delicacies like pigeon and rabbit." He gave me a sympathetic glance before continuing.

"I've spent some time going over the information I picked up at Hougoumont, you know." Arthur spoke more earnestly now. "That's why I haven't been by to see you for a while. Here is my theory: It seems that the boy noticed the rabbit hutches when they took him into the barn. When no one was looking, he opened one of them, intending to liberate the occupants. But the creatures—those that had survived the trauma, that is—were so terrorized, they couldn't budge. None of them emerged. So the boy grabbed the one that had caught his attention and slipped away, tucking the rabbit into his uniform jacket as he crossed the courtyard."

The one that had caught his attention . . . I regretted tuning Arthur out at that point, as his story was moving apace, but I'd felt a frisson at the mention of choosing a white rabbit from among its terrorized relatives, thereby saving it from neglect . . . or the dinner plate. The anecdote has an oddly familiar ring, doesn't it? There are people, it seems (thank heavens), who are naturally attracted to white rabbits.

"There was too much chaos and smoke for anyone to bother about a boy," Arthur went on. "Too many medical emergencies. So he carried the rabbit into the formal garden, and stopped about half-way across it, near the trellises."

At this point, Arthur meandered a bit from his plotline. He described the beauty of the Hougou-mont gardens, and how they had miraculously sur-vived the slaughter. Myrtle and fig trees were in bloom, he said. Jasmine and honeysuckle draped the trellises. Nature had been almost callous in her response to the violence, lacing the stench of cor-ruption with such sweet perfume.

In full swing now, Arthur embarked on a tale about how the British soldiers had butchered a pig the morning before the fighting started, and ate chunks of it warmed through over a fire and blackened with smoke. Finding his own portion too unsavory, Private Clay stuffed the meat in his pocket and went off to fight the French, after which, at the end of that long day, he found a fire burn-ing on some ruin or other and gladly extracted his pork for cooking. He discovered, however, "that the glow of fire arose from the half-consumed body of some party who had fallen in the contest."

I hesitated for a moment to give dramatic tim-ing its due. Then, impatient, I asked: "Where did the boy take the rabbit?"

"He just let him go," Arthur said.

"He . . . "

"Yes. He just set him down in the garden. But the animal didn't move from his side. Then someone yelled to him from the gate—maybe the young soldier, looking for him. The boy panicked and bolted, leaving the rabbit behind, and crawled through a tumbled-down section of the east wall, escaping into the orchard."

"Did the Allies on the ridge take him in?" I asked, my heartbeat accelerating. "Was he shot by a stray bullet?" *He may have perished finding his way off the battlefield,* Old Lavender had said. *Or died of fever.*

My ears grew chill.

"No one knows," Arthur answered.

"What happened to the rabbit?"

"It ran after the boy, apparently."

"How extraordinary!" I remembered Spode's story about the two-legged shape crossing the meadow by moonlight, followed by two four-legged shapes—one of them Old Lavender. But Spode's incident had occurred on the night before I left Hougoumont.

Arthur's story had happened two hundred years ago.

The French drummer boy had helped a white rabbit to freedom, then.

That still didn't explain who had liberated Old Lavender.

"Since the battle, white rabbits have apparently been spotted in the woods from time to time through-out the post-Waterloo generations," said Arthur, "all of them presumably descended from that creature the French boy liberated. Imagine that!"

He gave me a penetrating look. "I also learned that many years ago, someone escaped from your colony one night and spent several hours . . . well, let's just say *cavorting* . . . with one of those white descendants."

My heart raced. My haunches quivered. It would take a day to restore these functions to their normal rhythm. "*Old Lavender!*" I exclaimed.

Have you ever experienced a moment when everything rings at such a perfect pitch, it makes you dizzy? Well, here was my moment.

She returned just before dawn, Spode had said. *She was . . . changed, somehow.*

I'll say she was changed! And not just "some-how": she must have returned home pregnant! Thus it was that, through a single night of indis-cretion, a white rabbit surfaced occasionally in the colony, and our family perpetuated a noble Hou-goumont legend.

"History is like a wheel sometimes," Arthur said, deducing my thoughts. "It turns, and turns, and every once in a while a forgotten incident in the past makes a complete circle and reappears in some incarnation or other."

Arthur tilted his head at me with that signature panache of his. "You are one of those incarnations."

I suddenly had an overwhelming feeling of compassion towards our god. Funny, isn't it? I felt as if I could forgive Moon for his chronic tardiness, and the seemingly random way he went about his business, simply because the connecting threads of my own story seemed far too miraculous to have happened by chance. Something—*someone*—must have been involved.

I decided that the genius of a god is probably at its best with small miracles—the flames in the chapel of Hougoumont, for instance; or saving white rabbits—and not so impressive with bigger jobs, such as stopping wholesale slaughter.

In this rush of illumination, I even forgave myself for what had happened to Caillou. My guilt vis-à-vis the open gate evaporated. I thought of Old Lavender's famous maxim: *Should have, could have, would have . . . an inharmonious rhyme in any language, William. A thorny conditional everyone can do without. They should excise it from the grammar books.*

Old Lavender's teachings notwithstanding, Caillou himself had embraced the conditional occasionally, as the young tend to do. At their closest points, the French and Allied armies were only fifteen hundred yards apart, watching, waiting. They could smell each other's cooking fires; they could hear each other's songs. I know, I know, those aren't conditionals, they're the past tense, but here's what I'm getting at: "If everyone at Waterloo knew they were probably going to die," said Caillou, "they should have refused to fight. They could have talked about it, couldn't they? All those men and horses would have lived."

Not so thorny, in fact, that conditional: approximately fifty thousand men would have lived. And ten thousand horses.

And who knows how many rabbits?

⸪

"Where did you learn all this?" I asked Arthur, after I'd finished my mulling.

"Oh, you wouldn't believe the things that remain in the woods around Hougoumont," he said. "The resonance is quite astounding. Small creatures for miles around are still aware of the story."

Those who survived passed the experience on through collective memory . . . and resonance.

"Yes, but surely you must have talked to someone in the colony," I said. "To Spode, maybe?"

"Oh, Spode is gone."

I froze.

"It's true," Arthur said. "Everyone's gone."

I stared at him. I couldn't bear to ask if the farmer had finally carted my entire family off to the *marché*. Therefore, I asked the more palatable question: "Did they escape?" To which came the astonishing reply:

"Emmanuel let them all out. Last year."

Well, well, I thought, still staring at Arthur. Heroism certainly takes on many forms! I had heard that pregnant women dragged their husbands off the battlefield; I knew that mere boys played their drums in the thick of the fighting. Even oafish giants, therefore, can have their moment of glory.

Emmanuel had obviously known that Hougoumont's life as a farm was coming to an end, and that the rabbit colony would soon be hauled away to an uncertain fate. Well, maybe "known" is too strong a word. "Sensed," perhaps? Hang on: Does that mean that the boy had been harboring deeper waters all along, and even we, with our highly tuned sensibilities, hadn't noticed them?

It makes one wonder what had happened, exactly, on that day of liberation. Maybe providence itself had momentarily brightened the boy's wits and charmed his hand; maybe, as he passed by Hougoumont on his bicycle and experienced a dull firing of brain cells, that divine finger had brushed against his pudgy shoulder.

Bravo, dear Emmanuel! You spared us our own, inevitable Waterloo.

The dim-witted, liberating the meek . . . redemption had finally arrived at Hougoumont.

∴

Your head is probably spinning by now with the various untoward rabbit activities at Hougoumont. I know mine is. I don't usually make lists, as they remind me of Spode, but perhaps it would be clearer for everyone at this juncture if I did:

1) June 18, 1815: A French drummer boy released a white rabbit into the Hougoumont gardens.
2) About 165 years later: Old Lavender burrowed under the fence of the enclosure to tryst with a descendant of that white rabbit, and returned pregnant.
3) Some generations later—about twenty years or so—I was born.
4) Three years after that, Old Lavender left permanently, via the gate.
5) The next morning, I was taken away.
6) About seven years after all that, Emmanuel liberated the colony.

That's quite a lot of activity, now that I see it on paper. There are always loose ends, though, aren't there? Theories are never watertight; hutches never close cleanly (or vice versa). I'm thinking specifically of Activity No. 4. Spode had mentioned only vaguely "a two-legged shape." No clear description. A very long, loose end, one would say.

Who had liberated Old Lavender on the night before I was taken away?

Arthur was already primping himself in preparation for departure when I called him back down from the wall. "Who let Old Lavender out on the night before I left?" I demanded.

"Well," he said, obviously stalling. He glided onto the grass in an impeccable landing. "The gate had been opened, apparently."

"Yes, yes, I know that. But by *whom?*"

"A boy," Arthur said.

Emmanuel! Of course! So he *had* been held in too low regard. My innards relaxed and I sighed audibly. *Everything will be all right,* the boy had said as he loaded me into the banana crate. Maybe he'd noticed me frantically searching for Old Lavender, and was reassuring me that all would be well . . . *with her* . . . because he'd let her out himself the night before—possibly even watched her until she'd found a suitable hiding place in the meadow. If Arthur's story was to be believed, and the emboldened oaf Emmanuel had also let everyone else out seven years later, then liberation was clearly an important part of his destiny and we had all underestimated him cruelly.

"Fat and clumsy, was he?" I pressed Arthur, just to verify that Emmanuel had, indeed, been the unlikely hero, though my insides had seized up again. But then I remembered an indisputable fact about Emmanuel that my strained mental capacities momentarily overlooked, and that, when examined closely, tended to reduce the boy to his former, doltish dimensions:

Emmanuel never came to Hougoumont after dark . . . *never.*

I sighed again, but not with relief. I could see Emmanuel clearly in my mind, casting an anxious eye at the shadows lengthening over the Hougoumont meadow, throwing a handful of grain into the rabbit enclosure and lumbering off on his bicycle like a bear from a swarm of bees.

He just couldn't have come at night to liberate Old Lavender.

Arthur sensed my confusion. He sidled towards the begonias and dashed back again, as he often did when preparing an important thought. With altered tone he said, "Your grandmother . . . she . . . *saw things*, didn't she?"

The remark immobilized me. But perhaps not as completely as a question Old Lavender herself had asked, more than once: *Don't you ever see them, William?*

"Yes, she did see things," I muttered. "Well, she sensed them. Shapes. Movement. She called it 'the traffic of souls.'"

"Hmm," said Arthur. He fell silent, then continued: "In that case, it wouldn't surprise you to learn that the boy who opened the gate for your grandmother seven years ago, and led her across the meadow with her wild, white lover was slender, nimble."

Not Emmanuel, then.

"He was wearing a uniform."

But it had to be. There was no other explanation.

"And he carried a drum."

Author's Note

At this writing, Hougoumont Farm is at last being restored. The farmer passed away a few years after the liberation of William's family and the property was taken over by a consortium of local authorities. The hutch where William was born, and where his family continued to live after his departure to Brussels, has been razed, along with the antique dovecote. Neither structure figured in drawings of the farm from the Waterloo period.

These are cosmetic changes, however, and man-made: Nature did not join the consortium.

Go there and you'll see.

The three chestnuts still stand, though their vigil must surely be nearing its end. Their branches trace the battle's entire story against the sky, as if seeking redemption for the men buried at their feet.

The wind is laden with whispers and other, more precise sounds: the stamp of a horse's hoof, maybe. Or a tapping branch.

And if you're lucky, on days when the mists rise, you might see a flash of white near the eastern wall and wonder whether Hougoumont has just revealed one of its secrets.

William would be so pleased to know that it had.

∴

A veritable sea of books and essays has been written about Waterloo, though comparatively few of them go into any detail about Hougoumont. Publications that were particularly helpful for this story include: *A Narrative of the Battles of Quatre-Bras And Waterloo with the Defence of Hougoumont* by Matthew Clay; "Keep Hougoumont—at What Price?" by Mick Crumplin from www.waterloo200.org; "Waterloo Days" by Charlotte Eaton, from *Ladies of Waterloo: The Experiences of Three Women During the Campaign of 1815*; *Water-loo: A Guide to the Battlefield* by David Howarth; *Hougoumont* by Julian Paget and Derek Saunders; "Waterloo" by D. H. Parry, from *Battles of the Nineteenth Century, Vol. 1*; and *Le Goumont 1815: Citadelle de la mémoire* by Claude Van Hoorebeeck.

Acknowledgments

Unusual creative projects generally have few supporters at first . . . if any. People smile that smile, shuffle their feet and wish you well. Then the project dies. This paragraph, therefore, is short. But it's also the most important one in the book: Sarah McFadden, first-class editor and writer, you were brave enough to read the initial manuscript of *The Sage of Waterloo*, embrace it and offer some suggestions, without which I wouldn't have had the courage to send it to Norton and to you, Matt Weiland, editor extraordinaire. With insight and intuition you leapt into the

Untried, and for that I am deeply grateful. Cindy Gesuale, beloved childhood companion: nurturing small animals together imparted lessons of love, loss and friendship that inspire to this day. And for the occupants of my extended hutch, Francombe and Maxson alike: thank you! When I announced that I was going to write about rabbits and Waterloo, you guffawed (who didn't?). But seeing that I was serious, you indulged me, and encouraged me, and made me believe that providence would surely lend a hand.